"How do you go about making literature of
the unobtrusive life? Rune Christiansen offers up a patient
and quietly inexorable example in *The Loneliness in Lydia
Erneman's Life*. In Christiansen's story of a young woman
coming to grips with the most universal, most commonplace
trials of our existence, nothing is irrelevant, nothing is silent.
A lovely, enriching, compelling work of art."
—Michael Crummey, author of *The Innocents*

"*The Loneliness in Lydia Erneman's Life* is a
brilliant portrait narrated with tenderness, acuity, and
expertise. Like the best portraits, it doesn't reveal its subtexts
immediately. Rather, it beguiles us and shows the
colouring of a consciousness and how this palette shifts with
the surrounding phenomena and pressures—the influence
of strangers, seasons, pain, health, habits, dinners—this
ongoing flux of renewal, attachment, and demise."
—Moez Surani, author of *The Legend of Baraffo*

THE LONELINESS IN LYDIA ERNEMAN'S LIFE

RUNE CHRISTIANSEN

TRANSLATED BY KARI DICKSON

LITERATURE IN TRANSLATION SERIES

BOOK*HUG PRESS
TORONTO 2023

FIRST ENGLISH EDITION

Original text © 2014 by Rune Christiansen
First published as *Ensomheten i Lydia Ernemans liv* by Forlaget Oktober AS, 2014
Published in agreement with Oslo Literary Agency

English translation © 2023 by Kari Dickson

This translation has been made possible through the financial support of NORLA.

Library and Archives Canada Cataloguing in Publication

Title: The loneliness in Lydia Erneman's life / Rune Christiansen ;
    translated by Kari Dickson.
Other titles: Ensomheten i Lydia Ernemans liv. English
Names: Christiansen, Rune, 1963- author. | Dickson, Kari, translator.
Series: Literature in translation series.
Description: Series statement: Literature in translation series |
    Translation of: Ensomheten i Lydia Ernemans liv.
Identifiers: Canadiana (print) 20220457395 | Canadiana (ebook) 20220457425
    ISBN 9781771668347 (softcover)
    ISBN 9781771668354 (EPUB)
    ISBN 9781771668361 (PDF)
Classification: LCC PT8951.13.H45 E5713 2023 | DDC 839.823/74—dc23

Book*hug Press acknowledges that the land on which we operate is the
traditional territory of many nations, including the Mississaugas of the Credit,
the Anishnabeg, the Chippewa, the Haudenosaunee, and the Wendat peoples.
We recognize the enduring presence of many diverse First Nations, Inuit,
and Métis peoples and are grateful for the opportunity to meet, work, and
learn on this territory.

You will live far from your home and be happy.
—Edith Södergran

B efore all else, it should be said that Dagmar Erneman, mother of Lydia Erneman, almost drowned in her late teens when crossing a river on horseback. She had been out for a ride and was going to ford the river at the usual place, but the animal stepped into a hollow between the smooth stones and lost its balance. Dagmar fell under the heavy body, and as they floundered, she hit her head. She was found at dusk by two boys on their way home from a fishing trip. She was lying apparently lifeless on the bank, and the horse was beside her, neighing and pawing the ground with its hooves. It took the boys a few desperate minutes to heave her up across the saddle and take her back to the village. The episode took place in the fifties, in Frankrike in Jämtland, in the north of Sweden, but Dagmar's daughter, Lydia, did not hear about it until many years later, when she was nineteen and sitting eating with her parents. Her mother had set the table out on the terrace. They helped themselves to food straight from the pans and barely exchanged a word until Lydia announced, unexpectedly, that she was going to move. She had been offered a place at the Swedish University of Agricultural Science in

Uppsala down south and wanted to go, as her dream was to become a vet and work with horses, nothing else. Perhaps it was just natural concern, now that Lydia wanted to leave home, that caused Dagmar to grasp her daughter's hands across the table and tell her about this experience from her youth. Lydia looked at her mother and said she knew how to look after herself, but then her father, Johan, said so had her mother, she had been around horses since she learned to walk. Despite their opposition, when the autumn came around, Lydia Erneman left the family farm in Krokom. She drove all the way to Uppsala in the south and, in the years that followed, passed her exams with brilliant results. She scarcely had time for love, just the odd half-hearted affair, and days could pass between each time she saw her friends. This was not because she was shy or modest, but rather because she was consumed by her studies and the desire to be finished. She wanted to get on, she said, she wanted to work, she longed to fill her life with this work that she loved. She was neither restless nor unhappy in her own company. In fact, it was not unusual for her to think what a good life she had. Of course, she wished she had someone to share her every day with, someone to give herself up to, but this longing was not such that it diminished her existence in any way. She never had to fear being bored. Was she naive in her enthusiasm? No, she was not naive, she was rather level-headed and stubborn.

Her student years passed without Lydia losing patience for even a moment. She was a non-fighter where others struggled, and this irrepressible joy became her identity—her asset, for want of another word—and when she later applied for a job with the aging vet Carl Magnus Stangel, who ran a prestigious veterinary hospital just outside Tomelilla in Skåne, she already had glowing references from those who had known her at Ultuna, as well as an excellent degree. And Stangel, who trusted his instinct, employed Lydia immediately, almost as soon as he shook her hand. In the weeks that followed, he drove her around the flat, open landscape, so she would get to know the area, and him. It was, for the most part, Stangel who did the talking. Like an Eastern master he told his stories; he spoke at length about the eel's poisonous blood and the import of Holstein cattle to Skåne in the nineteenth century, he described his childhood in Småland and was more than happy to talk about the wild horses—also known as "the horses from the sea"—in the Camargue, where he had lived in younger years, and how wonderful and white they were. One story led to another, and it was the start of what would prove to be a few rich years for Lydia, there in Österlen. But when Stangel retired, Lydia applied for a job at a private veterinary practice in Norway. The clinic was in a rural location some way from the capital and was run by the vet Sigurd Brandt, a man who was in many ways like Stangel. Having shown Lydia around the district, or "parish," as he called it, he offered her the job. And so Lydia left southern Sweden and moved to the neighbouring country. She bought an old but well-maintained house with a mature Victorian-style garden, with flowers and herbs and berry bushes. There was also a greenhouse, and a wall to protect the garden from the northerly wind, but no lawn, which suited her fine; instead paved pathways wound between the beds, where everything grew with great vigour. The house was tall and white, with steep gables and a picket fence that ran around the not particularly large property. In spring and summer, grass pushed up against the painted wood, and in winter, the snow was left untouched. But now it was autumn, and orange and red leaves floated, swirled, and rustled in the wind. In October, a hint of melancholy came early on the light morning breeze, and yet Lydia often sat out on the small balcony, particularly in the evening, looking at old reference books or writing a kind of veterinary journal, in what was actually a simple, light blue unlined notebook. She could sit with these worthwhile tasks for hours. If she had a day off, she studied and made notes until dusk fell and the words were barely visible on the page. She swung her feet up onto the railing in the twilight and listened reverently to the constant rustling of the garden. She had a view of a couple of chestnut trees. They had grown tall and wide on either side of the gravel path that led down to the old main road. But every so often, a miserable or childish thought might disturb her. For example, she might get it into her head that her life was made up, that it wasn't really real. And it is here, following this rather hasty introduction, that the story of Lydia Erneman begins.

WHERE DOES
YOUR NAME
COME FROM?

One afternoon in late autumn, on her way home from an exhausting shift in a mucky, cold barn, Lydia stopped the car by the side of the road. She had been invited to dinner that evening and had anything but a good time, but right then she needed a few minutes in the fresh air. She pulled on the rubber boots she kept in the trunk, stepped carefully over the ditch, and tramped off through the boggy undergrowth. She stopped and stood quietly by the edge of a small lake, occasionally lifting a hand to wave off an insect, and a couple of times she reached out toward a dragonfly, not to catch it, more in recognition of a connection there in the dusk. That two creatures should share the same moment, be it ever so fleeting, was certainly not insignificant. Restless birdsong could be heard from the bushes, dry leaves rustled on the breeze, and everywhere the bracken and thistles and coltsfoot leaves nodded and swayed with sleepy, idle movements. Lydia bent down and put her hands into the water; they darkened and disappeared in a muddy cloud. She straightened up and dried her palms on her grey coat, which was already dirty. Even though she had inherited the coat from her mother,

Lydia used it for work in winter. She thought it seemed appropriate now that she and her mother were so far apart. It should not hang in a wardrobe as some kind of sentimental relic, it should be used until it was worn out. In precisely this way, she would use her mother's coat in her work and daily life.

She walked back to the car in the twilight. She did not have much time now to get home, have a shower, and change before going back out. She was not looking forward to it, as no matter how pleasant such evenings might be, she still felt uncomfortable, but it was one of her duties and to decline would be seen as stand-offish, or so Lydia thought, and the invitation had, after all, been well-intentioned; farmers, doctors, teachers, business folk and local politicians, the odd artist, all gathered to strengthen unity and tolerance in the local community. There were, of course, no rules for such gatherings, but Lydia had sensed a certain expectation from the organizers. She recognized it as soon as she received the small envelope with the invitation. It was written in a friendly but gently demanding tone, which she read as a request, something she was obliged to do.

During the meal, her thoughts wandered as she listened. Even in the middle of a conversation with the mayor, she was distracted and had to pull herself together. Was this a deeper reluctance surfacing? No, she dismissed the thought. She had always been careful to steer clear of any snobbery that made others' chat and carefree manners wearying and irrelevant.

When they left the table, she locked herself into one of the washrooms. For the first time in her life, she felt very alone, left to herself, and to be affected in this way was not like her, she who could enjoy all manner of small detail: the gentle presence she felt in nature, almost imperceptible and yet urgent and alive, when she was with the animals, by the edge of the lake at dusk, in a clearing in the forest—it was all she wished for. And she enjoyed a tussle with a stubborn and obstreperous horse.

It was almost a relief when she had to leave early, called out by Bråthen, one of the many farmers in the area. A stallion had ripped open his flank and needed to be looked at as soon as possible. She hastily said her thank-yous and goodbyes, sent a message to Brandt, and took a shortcut through the garden. It had rained, the grass was wet and the leaves and bushes were full of droplets, the trees were dripping, and the few berries that remained in the hedge that led down to the driveway where the cars were parked were dulled with the damp. She popped a couple in her mouth and sucked the juice. What did the bitter taste remind her of? She was unsure but decided it was some sort of poison and spat them out. Just then she heard footsteps on the gravel. It was one of the guests, a man. Lydia guessed he was in his mid-thirties. He explained that he had come by train from town and wondered if he could perhaps get a lift back to the station. Lydia was loathe to say no. She said he was welcome to a lift, but first she had to check on an injured horse at one of the farms. The man didn't mind the detour, he was just grateful not to have to walk all that way along the verge. They got into the car and Lydia turned the key. It was nice to have someone to talk to. She turned out onto main road. The man commented on how deserted it felt, and Lydia said you got used to it. She asked if he thought it was cold in the car and, without waiting for an answer, turned up the heating. There was something desolate about the ridge of the hills, something disconsolate, reminiscent of that pessimism that can strike at any moment, even in the company of friends.

When they got to the farm, a rather grand affair at the end of a golden-leafed birch avenue, the fog had descended and lay heavy and low. The yard was cobbled. Lydia got her rubber boots and overalls out from the trunk. She changed unabashedly into her work clothes. Her passenger stood by the open car door. He followed her movements like an awkward assistant, and Lydia suddenly remembered the first time she had gone to a farm on a not dissimilar errand, and old Stangel had had a blank expression on his face, and Lydia had understood that he was preparing himself for what was necessary, however unpleasant, and that the profession she had chosen was a respectable, if at times macabre, one. She realized she hadn't asked what her passenger was called, and nor had he asked her. And now they were standing on either side of the car, and even though Lydia had never smoked more than a couple of times at parties, she suddenly wanted a cigarette. She picked up her big black bag and headed toward the stable, where she shook hands with three men, one by one, as they more or less sprinted in.

The injured horse lay on his side, as though he had toppled over. He was shaking; his entire body was stiff and racked by cramps and spasms. The wound was so deep it cut through the muscle to reveal the intestines. She remembered a remark Stangel had once made, about how sensitive a horse's hearing was. She hadn't realized that the habit had formed so fast, but it was already part of her. She dropped to her knees to examine the animal and gave it a powerful dose of something to ease the pain. The men stood and watched her work in silence. When she eventually stood up and told them of her decision to put the animal out of its misery immediately, it prompted an uncouth response in the otherwise respectable stable, and one harsh word after another was flung at Lydia, while she, for her part, tried to defend herself against their irate faces with a mixture of infuriation and sympathy. She shrugged and shook her head. Bråthen threatened to sue her, he said she was incompetent and inexperienced, pointed a finger to her forehead and said she was finished there, then he marched out of the stable with the other two men at his heels. Lydia looked at the horse, a numbing fog filling her head. Once again, she dropped down on her knees. She pushed in the shiny, bluish intestines that were spilling out, then cleaned and stitched the wound. She pulled the dressing tight around the belly and back. The horse lifted his head in agitation and snapped at the air.

When she emerged out into the yard, she stopped. As though to make herself visible in the open space. There was something fundamentally wrong with the decision she had made. Everything in her rebelled, but Bråthen's threats had knocked her off balance. She was both absolutely certain and desperately unsure at the same time. The critical question was not if she had shown a lack of judgment in her decision, but rather if she had the right to defy the farmer's challenge. It was like being hounded by tormentors. She threw her bag and work clothes into the back of the car. Her passenger didn't say a word when she got in, it was as though there was a deeper connection, an accord, a respect between them. Lydia started the car and steered it round the mature tree that had been planted long ago in the middle of the yard to protect the farm. They left the farm and the avenue of bare trees behind and pulled out onto the main road again. The mist had thickened, visibility was appalling, now and then a yellowish light flared as an oncoming car snailed past in the opposite direction. A while later, they were able to make out the shape of a copse, and this eased Lydia's growing anxiety. When her passenger looked at her, she took it to mean he was looking for an answer in her face. She said quickly that he should still be in time to catch his train.

At the station, Lydia offered to wait with him until the train came, in case it had been delayed or cancelled, a friendly gesture the passenger breezily dismissed with a wave of his hand, but then thanked her for, when she insisted. He dashed out to buy a ticket from the machine, stood there in the drizzle, and tapped on the broken glass windshield to no avail, he achieved nothing more than to get wet. When he opened the passenger door, the cold air blasted in, and no sooner had he sat back down and closed the door than the windows steamed up. He apologized and said that this was more trouble than she needed on top of everything else. Lydia barely heard him.

She had to put the horse down. She said this out loud, though mostly to herself. She had allowed herself to be swayed. She had given in to those fools. Her passenger said that if she was thinking of going back to the farm, he would go with her. Lydia looked at him, but before she even had time to protest, he repeated what he had said. She thought it was perhaps madness in the mist, to drive slowly back, but there was no other way.

As they approached the farm for a second time, the passenger told her, as though it was finally required, that his name was Edvin, and Lydia introduced herself in return. They went into the stable together, and even though it was obvious, if not spoken, Edvin asked her what she intended to do. She put her bag down on the concrete floor and nodded toward the door; she wanted to be alone with the animal and with her duties. She got out the necessary equipment, looked at her watch to register the time. A dull anguish spread through her.

When the fatal act was done, she observed her work and felt peace again. She phoned Brandt, apologized for interrupting the party, but asked him to come all the same. Then she walked across the yard to tell Bråthen.

She had been in the stable with the farmer, who was now silent and composed, for little more than half an hour when Brandt arrived in a taxi, and he could confirm that Lydia's decision was justified, indeed necessary. He got straight to the point and told Bråthen that Lydia had done the only compassionate thing and he should have understood that, that anything else would only prolong the poor animal's suffering, then he diplomatically explained to Lydia that it was perfectly understandable that Bråthen did not want to lose such a beautiful and valuable animal. Not much more was said. The dead horse lay there, a sorrowful sight; Lydia held out her hand, Bråthen shook it and mumbled something about the animal looking so alive.

BREAD DIPPED
IN TEA

T hat night, Lydia dreamed she was home on her parents' small farm. She was of indefinable age, not a child, not a teenager, not an adult, but rather all of these ages at once. She stood in the yard in the pouring rain, looking down at a small pool of water. No matter how hard her father tried or how much he worked on the drainage, small, shallow puddles always formed in the gravel outside the barn, and now, in her sleep, Lydia was unusually taken with this small pool, because the surface was as smooth as a mirror, even though it was raining. How was that possible? Lydia thought, or dreamed that she thought: One always returns, it's necessary. And then she said, "Come, let's go," to no one in particular, and woke up straightaway.

The sounds from the kitchen filled her with slim and short-lived relief. The passenger, this Edvin, had kept her company through the early hours of the night. He had asked her in the car if she would like someone to stay with her, and she said she would appreciate that, and in all the confusion she had welcomed a stranger into her house. She showed him how the sofa in the guest room upstairs could be folded out to make a bed, and once she had given him a duvet and a woollen blanket, she thanked him and said goodnight.

At the breakfast table, which had been set with the basics—two plates, two mugs, some bread and cheese, a pot of tea—Lydia asked Edvin what he did for a living, and he told her he was currently an actor at the national theatre. Lydia quickly drank some tea as though she was out of time, but then she felt unsure about what he meant by "currently." And as he dipped a piece of bread and cheese in his tea, Edvin explained that in his youth he had decided not to commit to any one job for more than three or four years at a time. He had been a lumberjack, a train conductor, a baker and a diver, worked in a plastic factory, been a guide and a verger. His first job had been as a fireman in a village in Portugal, through a summer and an autumn. He spent eight hours a day up a tower keeping an eye out for smoke on the forested slopes. It required great concentration, there was no time to read or study, he alternated between standing and sitting, he sang to himself or took a CD player with him so he could listen to music, which did not require his attention. And then, as though there was a connection, he asked if Lydia knew that around 90 percent of all silent films had been ruined, lost forever, and somewhat cryptically followed this up by saying he did not like turning up anywhere unannounced, even when he knew the hosts, even when they were his close friends. He spoke calmly, it was like the unfolding of a story, seen from different angles and ever changing, as though the fragments did not have a shared source. When he was thirteen, he had run away with the circus, he said. For some years in his youth, he had lived in a small place at the north end of Østerdalen, and every summer a circus visited the mountain village. As soon as the sluggish trailers rolled down the main street, on their way to the playing field that was a stone's throw from his house, he was there, ready for hire. Not that there was any pay to be had, only a few measly tickets and free popcorn, but that was temptation enough and the work was simple: he carried buckets of water to the animals, covered the ground in the big top with sawdust, and stapled posters onto notice boards and poles: "World-Class Artists," "Two Nights Only," "Exotic Animals from Every Continent." Lydia listened, and when Edvin had finished his tea and stood up, when they once again found themselves in the car, on the way to the train station, she felt it was incumbent upon her to say how much pleasure his visit and kindness had given her. She spent the journey mulling over how to express herself, but when they arrived at the station, the train was already waiting at the platform, and even though Edvin was attentive and thanked her, Lydia was not able to say what she wanted, she lifted her hand in a clumsy farewell, and that was that.

When she got home, she went out to hang the washing in the back garden. The whirligig washing line started to spin as she pegged up the bedclothes, the metal whined, and a sudden gust danced off with the duvet cover, which she clearly had not pegged well enough. She gathered it up, stood for a while looking at the hills to the west, the fading morning pinks, the sun no more than a suggestion behind the clouds. She was suddenly aware of how thin her clothes were, that she had sat like this in the car, stood like this in the station, with her breasts bare under the fabric of her dress.

A WOMAN
CROSSES A FIELD
IN THE SNOW

Lydia sat huddled in a chair in the living room. She still had her coat on, and the collar was turned up as though to protect her from the cold. The working day was over. There had been nothing exceptional about it. What had she experienced? She had removed burs from a long-haired collie's coat, she had surgically removed a growth on a horse's ear, cleaned wounds, written prescriptions, and overheard a number of conversations that were irrelevant to her. Two farmers had spoken at length about the tragedy in Tiszaeszlár, a terrible affair that apparently took place in Austria-Hungary in 1882. Lydia was not sure whether they had read the same book or seen the same TV program, and wondered why on earth they were talking about it, it seemed so upsetting, but she was caught up in her duties as a vet and it was not possible to escape. While she rinsed her boots out in the yard of another farm, a man had been holding forth on the qualities of different apple varieties, and when she got back to the clinic, two girls had come in with a rabbit each, and even though Lydia's shift was long since over, she had a look at the animals, a quick examination, offered some friendly advice on changing the animals' diet, she had enjoyed spending the short half-hour with the two tense and silent children.

It started to snow as soon as she left the clinic, a white curtain in the falling dusk. When she got to her car, a boy was standing there who just stared at her. He didn't say a word, he seemed hesitant, reluctant to interrupt. It was not until Lydia asked how she could help that he stuttered in a nervous voice that he knew, as he put it, about a dog that had been run over, he had left it in a hut in the woods. Lydia had long since given up keeping strict working hours, so she told him to hop in the car and said she would take a look at the dog. Office hours, how was that possible?

There was not much to be done for the dog, the kindest thing would have been to put it down straightaway, but with the horse drama still fresh in her mind, Lydia decided to wait, without a doubt, more for the boy's sake. She gave the animal an injection, not enough to kill it, but nearly, then bandaged its right front leg; she cleaned the wounds with such care as to give hope to someone who might not know better. She put her hand on the boy's shoulder and said they should let the dog rest now, for a day or two at least, if not three. She promised to come by and check on it every day.

Outside the hut, which lay in a tight cluster of trees, the evening was so beautiful that Lydia wanted to comment on it, but it was not the time for waxing lyrical. Instead, she asked what the boy was called. His name was Johan. And Lydia told him that that was also her father's name. She drove Johan back to the house where he lived, stopped the car alongside the fence.

Soon after, she was home herself and could sink down into the chair. An insect had managed to get in on the wrong side of the window, a small greyish moth out of season. It bumped against the glass in desperation, here then there, as though it had forgotten its instinct.

The next morning, Lydia went to look in on the dog. It was lying in the same position as when she had left the day before, and its breathing was irregular and weak. So it was not over yet, there was still life in the battered body. Johan had been there, he had put out a bowl of water and left a crust of bread on the floor. Lydia did what she had to do and went outside. There was always plenty to look at in a copse like this: the slender trunks, the tangled undergrowth, the dappled light and rowan berries that were now shrunken and black. It was these unassuming things, these small details, that appealed to Lydia, they seemed to allow her small glimpses of her childhood, as though it still secretly existed within her. For the first time since she was a student, she was caught by a wave of homesickness. She pictured her father. He was walking down the road, sauntering. Nothing about his face had changed. He stopped by the old hawthorn hedge. She wanted to call to him but was unsure how to behave. One only sees what one is, she thought, but that was no reason to despair. Was it not in connection with Japanese paper houses that the expression "the unshakable foundation" was used?

At the end of the working week, she was invited to Sigurd Brandt's home. She was tidying in some drawers in the laboratory when Brandt stuck his head in from the dark corridor and said it was high time she came to meet his family. And so it was that no more than an hour later she sat down at the table with her boss, his wife, Ruth, and Arne, their after-thought. Everything in Brandt's home whispered stability. They were served pork chops in a rich balsamic sauce, an excellent meal, but Lydia was not used to such strong flavours and it gave her a slight stomach ache. She drank water, but it didn't help. She noticed that Ruth called her husband by his last name: "Brandt is good at making food," "Brandt has said many favourable things about you," "Brandt never watches television." Fortunately, the conversation around the table flowed well. There was great amusement when Lydia told where she was from, the town that could be a country in the north of Sweden. The different topics slipped seamlessly into each other. Brandt and Ruth talked about how hard the winters could be in this part of the country, about their son's schooling, and about their two daughters, who had long since moved out, one had studied in Australia, while the other had married and settled in Trondheim. Ruth mentioned Bråthen's horse. She commended Lydia for her decision and said they were all idiots. Lydia thanked her for her support, though she was not sure if Ruth meant farmers in general were idiots, or if the characterization applied to the horse owners in partic-ular, and then hastened to say that it was never easy. One is, of course, likely to take it badly if one loses an animal.

After the meal, they stayed at the table and played cards. It struck Lydia that the Brandt family had given her insight into something solid and indestructible. She imagined the small group in all manner of daily situations, and thus realized that she herself was a typical single woman, in that all her interests and how she chose to spend her time might possibly surprise others. But Brandt and his wife seemed to appreciate her company, and even the twelve-year-old stayed with them. It was after midnight when Lydia got up to leave. Brandt followed her out to the door, thanked her for coming, and said she could drop by whenever she felt like it. He gave her a hug and stood waving as she drove off.

On the way home, Lydia decided that she would go to see the dog again. She parked the car by the side of the road and set off across the snowy fields in the direction of the copse. Everything around her shimmered in the cold, clear moonlight. Once inside the hut, she hunkered down beside the lifeless creature. She felt its nose. A gentle warmth dampened her palm, and the animal whimpered. Delighted by this unexpected turn of events, she stood up. A lock of hair came loose, and she tried to push it back, without success. She thought it would have been good to have company right now, if only Edvin could have been there, he would have seen what she could do. It was a fuzzy response. She had been so downcast that evening with the horse. But Edvin had proved to be a patient man, and that was exactly what she needed, the affirmation a level-headed stranger could give. She knew she was trusting her first impression from that evening. What else could she do? It was pointless to try to conquer something that constantly evaded her.

The very next day, Johan came into the clinic with the dog. Without warning, he was suddenly standing there in the doorway to Lydia's office, with the dog beside him. The boy declared solemnly that it was no longer injured, because Lydia had fixed it. Lydia bent down and ran her hand along the dog's back, she checked its leg and, sure enough, it was healing nicely, given the circumstances. She put a hand on Johan's shoulder. She got the feeling that the boy imagined she had sorted out all the details in some great plan, but the truth was that she had set the animal on its way to death, albeit with a hairline margin. She was reluctant to take all credit for the miracle, but she nodded so as not to upset the boy and said that together they had got the dog back on its legs, and that was truly a feat. Johan smiled. He said he wanted to name the dog after Lydia's father. Lydia nodded. She noticed that he had a small white scar on his chin. She put her finger on it. Johan's cheeks flushed and he looked down with crossed eyes, as if he wanted to see if she had something hidden in her hand.

TWO POINTS
OF GRAVITY

Following a cloudless day, it started to snow again. Lydia lay on the brown leather sofa in the living room, her head back over the edge of the arm, her hands under her neck, a very uncomfortable position, but she didn't move, she just looked at the white flakes falling thick and fast outside. Once again she found herself thinking about her father, and once again she pictured him walking along the road. She could see his face clearly, his beautiful man's face, weathered by the sun and cold air, broad cheekbones, broad nose, the scar on his chin barely visible under his stubble, and his grey eyes that looked at her impatiently, as though searching for their own lost brilliance. He lit a cigarette. It reassured her. The picture of him with a cigarette in his mouth always reassured her, made her cheerful, as in childhood. She had once overheard a conversation between him and her mother, he had said something like paternal love required distance, as distance built trust, he believed. It often seemed that when her father spoke, it was with the inherent certainty that he was right. He often said: "I don't need to look at the clock to know what time we live in." What had her mother replied? What had she said?

Lydia could scarcely remember. This was possibly because Lydia had always been wary of her mother, even as a child. At a young age, she had understood that her mother was racked with anxiety and cried easily. "To be at peace with oneself" was her mother's thing. But "to be at peace with oneself" was, to all intents and purposes, the same as denying that one was part of everything else—all the important and banal things you went through, the big and small disruptions that helped to strengthen you, perhaps even liberate you. Sometimes, caught as she was between these two ways of living, Lydia felt like a traitor without being able to say why. Already as a child, she had thought that her mother and father's marriage was based on the agreement that some things remained unsaid, and that this form of coexistence was synonymous with an inalienable and accepted distance, a detachment and an absence. In many ways, her mother and father lived their own lives and did separate things, had separate interests and separate pleasures. But they shared their worries and woes, side by side they weathered all storms, united as one. Was it not Napoleon who Bergson quoted when he said that the transition from tragedy to comedy is effected simply by sitting down?

THE ENAMEL DISH

Lydia decided to go home to see her parents. Why this decision suddenly felt so urgent, she didn't know. No one had invited her, nothing had enticed her, and the season was not conducive to long road trips. But no matter how things were or were not, as soon as she had a few days off, she packed a suitcase, filled a thermos with coffee, and settled in behind the wheel. As she turned the key in the ignition, she remembered something that had happened when she was a child. A minor incident. It was summer. She came into the living room. She had a tiny, unripe apple in her hand. Her father was standing by the window. He glanced briefly over toward the door and mumbled something almost to himself, as if he had not seen her, as if she was not something one might notice. She thought: Is he not cold standing there, even though he's in the direct sun? She turned on her heel and hurried out of the room, out of the house, and, overcome with embarrassment, she threw the small, unready fruit onto the compost heap behind the barn. Lydia was taken aback that this silly memory popped up now. The pitiful meaning was obvious, and the incident itself contained a sadness one could easily recognize and be done with. She ran through the radio stations, and only when she found one that played classical music did she fasten the seat belt and reverse out onto the road.

Late in the evening, as she approached the farm, driving slowly through the thick snow, she felt so heartsick that she found it hard to breathe, and she didn't know why. It was not nostalgia, and she didn't even feel homesick, not really. On the occasions that she did plan to visit her parents, it was rather like the kind of mechanical movement one makes when one follows the pattern on wallpaper with a fingertip but then eventually gives up, turns over with indifference, and falls back to sleep. No doubt her father had hoped she would take over the farm one day; even when she moved away to study, he had hinted at the opportunities that lay ahead if she was only sensible and chose to take on the farm after him. Her mother was more ambiguous, careful to point out that she understood her husband, but it was clear, to Lydia at least, that she was also delighted by her daughter's abilities and desire to travel. Perhaps her mother had thought: Lydia has her own life. Or had they both assumed that she would one day find her way back to what had once been? As though time were a given quantity after all, fluid and immutable at the same time.

Lydia drove the car into the garage. She felt warm around the eyes, and her throat was sore. She took the suitcase out from the back seat and walked across the yard. There was a light in the kitchen window. A tall figure stood leaning toward the glass, looking out. It had to be her father. He disappeared, and moments later the door opened. He stood there in the warm glow of the outside light and seemed to weigh himself down. Lydia stopped in front of him, put down her suitcase. He held out his hand, but Lydia was having none of it, she opened her arms and hugged him. He asked where she was heading, of all things. Lydia didn't know what to say. God, how ridiculous, she thought. It was though she had to muster all her strength to defend herself against these standard phrases. Her father picked up the suitcase, and they went in. She kept her coat on. He asked if she was well and if she was happy to take her old room. She nodded, and he tramped up the stairs with her luggage. She whispered after him to ask if her mother was asleep, but he didn't hear. A door creaked upstairs, then there was silence. Lydia went into the living room. It all seemed so incredibly alien, unfamiliar and impregnable. This brief, uneventful moment did not worry her, but it was unnerving that along with other big and small things that had happened in the past few weeks, it perhaps formed a connection and a continuity, as though a plan existed. She let her finger glide over the sideboard, the dark hard wood. The key still lay in a turquoise enamel dish, it was tarnished and black now, just one small turn and everything would finally be explained or refuted. Lydia picked it up, weighed it in her hand, but then immediately put it back. As a child, she had often stood there and imagined what lay hidden behind the varnished doors, a treasure perhaps, a valuable stone taken from the depths of the earth, or bloodied stolen goods, jewellery snatched from the hands of the dead. She stood there for a long time, finding it hard to breathe normally. Why had she

45

never opened the mysterious piece of furniture to discover what was actually stored inside? Everything in the house was so real, so tangible, nothing was light or impractical, everything had a purpose, and all tasks had a dignity and a weight.

Her father came down the stairs. He switched on the ceiling light. Again Lydia asked about her mother, and again it seemed that he didn't hear. He looked at her in astonishment. He said, "Goodness," then assured her that all was well with her mother, she was asleep, she had been extremely tired for a few weeks now, as she often was in winter, probably best not to wake her, but she would no doubt be thrilled to see Lydia at the breakfast table in the morning.

Other than wishing each other good night, the father and daughter said nothing more. Lydia lay awake in the bed under the sloping ceiling. She lay there and felt the tender warmth of a fever in her body. The curtains were not fully drawn, so she could look out at the snow. She thought about Edvin. He had been so straightforward, there was something unforced about him that had made an impression on her. She was slightly disappointed that she had not heard from him, but there was no point in dwelling on it. And yet she could not *not* dwell on it. Maybe he was lying awake too, maybe he was lying awake staring at the ceiling and thinking of her. He was probably asleep, he was probably asleep beside a woman, his woman, his beloved of many years, and a deep peace reigned between them, and he turned onto his back and sought a more comfortable position for his shoulders and neck. Then she remembered that he had said she was like Ingrid Thulin in the role of Mr. Aman. She had forgotten to ask what he meant. She had not seen Ingrid Thulin as a man. And she was not particularly masculine, was she? Nor was Lydia. But she had understood that it was a compliment. She tried to recall Edvin's face in as much detail as possible, but his features kept slipping away.

LIKE THE FICKLE
SOUL THAT SHE WAS

A faint scent of carnations filled the room, and her mother's breathing as she slept was so uninhibited that it brought to mind anxiety. During breakfast, her father had explained that he had chosen not to say anything to Lydia about Dagmar's condition so as not to worry his daughter so late at night, and that it was nothing serious anyway, so there was plenty of time to tell her in the morning. Lydia had at first been upset by this omission, but she soon realized that he had acted with the best intentions. She took a cup of coffee upstairs and sat down on the chair beside her mother's bed, and when her mother woke sometime later and saw her daughter sitting there, she sat up in bed and bumped the bedside table, causing the water in the glass to create a dancing reflection on the wall above her head. Lydia moved to sit on the edge of the bed and asked what was wrong with her. Her mother straightened her nightdress and said it was nothing in particular, she was just feeling a bit unwell. But Lydia persisted. She wanted to know if the doctor had been to see her. Of course the doctor had been there, and there was nothing to worry about. Dagmar lifted her arm and put it affectionately around her daughter's shoulder. Lydia was so beautiful, she said, her skin so smooth and warm. Once again Lydia fixed her eyes on the quivering reflection above the head of the bed. But it's true, her mother insisted. Lydia should have been on the stage, she was so beautiful. And then her mother turned her focus to something else. Could Lydia remember when they used to listen to radio plays together? Yes, Lydia remembered. She remembered it with joy. Radio plays, they were what was available in the provinces. When Lydia was a teenager, the mother and daughter frequently settled down by the radio and listened while they drank tea or hot chocolate. The old radio plays from the fifties and sixties, in particular, made an impression on Lydia. Listening to the warm, well-articulated voices of Gunnar Björnstrand, Eva Dahlbeck, Jarl Kulle, Gertrud Fridh, Annika Tretow, Max von Sydow, Catrin Westerlund, and Anita Björk inspired a special kind of peace. All the images had stuck with her; from foreign countries and bygone eras, from airy interiors to rambling fantasies: the room smelled of lily of the valley, didn't it? And the village steeple that towered up from the ridge of the hill. The frozen water carrier with the iron scoop, what became of him? And Medea's machinations, were they not cunning and tragic? And that old devil Tartuffe, didn't the loathsome man appear in person only in the third act? And what must Madame Ranevsky have thought when the cherry orchard was chopped down?

Lydia stood up and went over to the window. Great mounds of snow, a cold sun, and mountains and forest. Her father was busy clearing the yard. He sat hunched over the tractor steering wheel. A shadow. Slow, wide circles around the birch tree. What was it, Lydia wondered, that made him so reticent? That was the puzzling thing about her father. It was as though he was cheerful by nature, but it never shone through, as though something big and brooding blocked the joy. Lydia noticed how tense she was herself. She turned back to look at her mother, asked if she should make her some coffee. With a heavy movement, Dagmar shifted her hips and sat up in bed. She grabbed hold of her daughter. It was so good to feel how confident and strong she was. Had she found herself a man in Norway? Lydia nodded. She had found a beautiful and hard-working man, she said. He was a bit older than she, but not so much that it mattered. Then she told her mother about the white house, and about her simple life there, about Johan and the dog, and about the girls in the house next door who spent hours every Sunday grooming the horses on one of the neighbouring farms, and said that her mother no doubt understood that her passion for animals often resulted in intense and engrossing work. These few glimpses of her daily life were sketched and abandoned in all haste. Dagmar listened as if something of great importance had been clarified, the kind of clarity one experiences when, as a child, one is told that the Virgin Mary in the Bible was visited by an angel who told her she was with child.

The next morning, Lydia went for a walk along the road. The first stretch along the fields was straight and deserted. Despite all the snow, Lydia imagined she could still smell traces of wood and other forestry activities. A car sped past, and then another, but the second car then braked and stopped, waited. When Lydia came up alongside it, the window rolled down and a woman stuck her head out. She asked if she could give Lydia a lift anywhere. Lydia'a first instinct was to say no, but then she changed her mind and said yes, please, after all. She got into the car, and they shook hands. The woman was called Eivor, and even though she was around Lydia's age, the two had never met. Lydia said she was on her way to the shop. But the shop was in the opposite direction, Eivor said, and it was a fair way to walk. Lydia tapped the heel of her hand to her forehead. How could she forget that? Eivor waved this off and gestured that it wasn't a problem. She turned the car in a passing place and said she could drop Lydia off at the shop. Was Lydia Erneman's daughter, by any chance? Yes, Lydia was Erneman's daughter. Eivor said that they had heard about Dagmar. That it was so sad. Lydia looked at her, horrified to begin with, but then nodded in acknowledgement, not wanting to make things difficult and awkward for the kind woman. It was a good thing that Lydia had come. You never knew how quickly things might progress. Lydia turned her head away, looked out through the window. There was nothing there for her, nothing was recognizable. She was angry and had to hide it as best she could. Fortunately, it did not take long to drive to the shop. The large, barrack-like building emblazoned with neon-coloured signs seemed to stand there flashing in the snow. Eivor said she would wait. It really was not much fun to wander along the narrow roads, she said.

Lydia bought the local paper, a loaf of bread and milk and bananas, so she could fill a carrier bag and make her errand look believable. Back in the car, she thanked Eivor for her patience. She wondered how she might tease out of the woman what was actually wrong with her mother. To keep the conversation flowing, she said it was no doubt beautiful up by the power plant these days, so she might try to get up there for a ski.

Eivor stopped on the road by the farm. Lydia thanked her once again. She took the bag of groceries and walked up to the house, then stamped the snow off her shoes. Before she went inside, she took a deep breath. Apart from the ticking of the grandfather clock in the hall, the house was silent. She remembered that her father had once said that she expected too much, that her head buzzed more than a wasps' nest. Perhaps that was true, she thought; one imagines so much, but then one tires of the fantasies and gives up.

Her father had lit the fire. He was sitting in the worn, wingback armchair, his back to her, and seemed to be asleep. Lydia went into the kitchen and peeled a banana. Her parents were old now, she thought. But their marriage really did give a sense of security. It was as though they each individually expressed what burdened them both, as though they had a shared purpose. As a child, she had never thought her parents were bored, there was always something energetic about the life they lived on the farm. And in the evenings, out on the veranda in summer, or in front of the fire in winter, there was always a kind of quiet accord in their conversations; even when they sat in silence there was something accepting and conciliatory between them.

Lydia went into the living room. Her father was still sitting completely motionless. The black-sooted fireplace gaped at the room. The logs were barely smouldering. She remembered the boy she had read about at school, who was visiting his grandparents and who lay awake at night and got it into his head that his grandfather was dead, so he crept in to him in the dark and felt for the old man's neck. How would her father cope without Dagmar? What rules would define his every day when she was gone? One could not simply submit to oblivion. Johan turned toward Lydia, befuddled as though he had just woken from a bad dream. He asked in a thick voice where she had been. Lydia said she had gone for a walk, in an attempt to shake the remains of her fever. As soon as she said it, she heard how ridiculous it sounded. She confronted her father. Was Dagmar seriously ill? Her father stood up. He looked at his daughter. On the wall above the fireplace, just behind his head, hung a hunting rifle and an old cartridge bag in dark leather. He put his hand on her shoulder and said it was true that her mother was ill, but it was nothing to worry about. She was improving every day. He stroked her cheek and disappeared out into the hall. She heard him step into his boots, and a moment later the front door opened. She felt tired. She went up to see her mother, but her mother was asleep. And outside, the wind had blown up and whistled around the corners of the house, whipping the snow in sharp gusts across the yard. Lydia liked summer best, she always had. When she could wade through the ferns and thistles, her head full of myriad dreams. And she loved to climb the steep hillside from the small woods up to where the trees had been cleared and where new shoots were already in evidence; to think that these would grow into colossal trees with leafy crowns that almost filled the sky, as they did when she was a girl lying on a grassy bank with her hands behind her head. As a teenager, she often lay down just to breathe and think and dream. But always at the same place, where the riverbed narrowed and forked into two smaller rivers. She thought that, in many ways, this was her source, her beginning. After all, everything had to have a beginning, everything was created, every living thing gathered energy and strength in order to gain time. She used to lie there on the warm forest floor and feel that this was how it was meant to be, and in a kind of prayer, she would lift her hand and rest it on her chest, as though in preparation, as though she did not quite trust the oxygen she breathed. Lydia rested her forehead against the glass. Her father was standing at attention in the snow, stoic and frail at the same time. He had his back to her and seemed to be fiddling with something. And sure enough, a flashlight was turned on and the pale beam tipped up to the treetops behind the tool shed, then was lowered and sailed slowly over the fields. What was he trying to illuminate? It was not rare for them to see wolf tracks in the snow around the farm, particularly in prolonged cold patches. Lydia breathed condensation onto the glass. She felt at peace. As though a long and equitable battle had been won.

THE JOURNEY
THAT TOOK
A THOUSAND YEARS

N ext to her mother's grave was a mound of black soil and clumps of frozen clay. Lydia held her father's arm. The people from the local community stood with bowed heads. Lydia recognized only a few of them: Eivor and a couple of old family friends. The minister said his piece, it was moving, there under the grey sky, but strangely, none of those present shed a tear. The coffin was lowered with the help of two sturdy ropes, and one of the pallbearers, an old man with sinewy hands, struggled to hold on, he was pulled forward on the slippery ground, until someone then sprung to his aid and a fiasco was averted.

At the wake, which Johan held at home on the farm, ham hock and cabbage with lots of pepper was served along with aquavit and water. If one was going to express gratitude to a person who had just passed on, one should thank them for their efforts, thought Lydia, where she sat at the head of the table. She did not say this out loud, but raised her glass to her father, and he gave her a nod and emptied his. His face emanated a confused and wan misery.

Lydia returned home to Norway only a few days after the funeral. She was unsure, at first, whether her father needed her or not, but soon dismissed the thought. All Johan spoke about was what was going to happen with the farm. Caught as he was in his grief and rigid ideas, he went around muttering that he would no doubt manage, his daughter could just go, as he had never depended on anyone for help. These poorly disguised reproaches bothered Lydia, but she decided to leave all the same. She cleaned and tidied the house, packed her things, and on her way out, she gave Johan a hug, which he accepted reluctantly. As she closed the door behind her, she thought she heard a cold and angular echo. There was no sun to speak of on that winter day, but a patch of blue sky had opened, and while it did not lift her mood entirely, it did make her feel a little less dejected. She got into the car, glanced up at the rearview mirror. Her father was standing looking out from the kitchen window.

She had thought of driving all the way south without stopping but was forced to pull over just north of Hamar, as she needed gas. And while she was standing at the pump, her father rang. In a thick voice, he explained that he needed a friend, someone who believed in him and did not think he was a bad person. Lydia realized she was trembling. Should she turn around and drive back? She didn't know how to respond to him. He said he needed her to think well of him. That everything had been so diffuse recently, he continued, and under different circumstances, her visit would have been a blessing. Lydia pulled the collar of her coat up against the bitter wind. She put the cap back on the tank and went to pay. They could talk more later.

When she returned to the car, a squirrel was sitting on the hood. As though suddenly alerted to danger, it whipped up the windshield and across the car roof, jumped down between the pumps, and darted across the open ground. It stopped and sniffed the air. A truck pulled in from the road and rolled slowly through the slush. In an attempt to save the squirrel, Lydia lurched forward. She slipped and the vehicle hit her. It propelled her backwards and she landed on her spine in the slush. The impact itself was not so great, but she banged her head against a concrete edge. Dazed, she stood up and brushed the snow from her coat. She swallowed the spit that had pooled in her mouth. It was viscous and tasted of iron. She looked down at her palms, they were smeared with blood, her sleeves stained and her eyes unfocused. Something was ringing close to her ears. A man came running toward her. She toppled forward and was not able to stop herself. She dreamed that she was having a wash and put her face under the tap to rinse it; she stood there for a long time, until her skin was red and cold. Her mother was talking to her. There was strange resonance to her voice. Lydia must not forget to visit her father at Christmas. It was required, wasn't it? Dagmar bent close to her ear and whispered that now that the great struggle was finally over, Lydia must not forget that she had slept on a good mattress, a spring mattress, it was so comfortable. Lydia was in her childhood home. She went through all the rooms, stopped and looked at each object. The sunlight filtered through the thin curtains. After all the rain, the summer warmth smelled of intense growth, and the slim birch trunks were up to their knees in water in the ditch alongside the road. She pushed open a door and emerged into the back garden. The rain dripped from the trees, drops as big and shiny as marbles. Her mother was sitting in a wicker chair. She looked at her daughter with affection and said her name: Lydia. Lydia. Her thoughtless darling. She was a beautiful girl, if a little too thin. How was her father going to manage now?

Silence falls on the vale.
The tired birds fall asleep.
My heart, after all the day's struggles,
You have found your peace.
The night's overwhelming
Silence without a name
Envelops me with a mother's arms,
With a tender kiss.

Lydia opened her eyes. A blanket had been laid over her shoulders. She felt embarrassed. Sharp snowflakes pricked her face. A stranger helped her to her feet. He brushed her hair back with his hand. A heavy, coarse hand. He was shaking, he spoke to her, his voice shook too. Shadows and silhouettes swayed around him.

While she waited in the hospital for the doctor to show her the X-rays, Lydia recalled that Superman could not go near any fragments from his home planet, Krypton. Was that not because if he touched the glowing green crystals, he would lose his supernatural power and almost certainly die? The room was austere. A faint gurgling and sigh came from the radiator under the window. She was in no state to work out how much time had passed since the absurd incident at the gas station. From where she was sitting, she could see it was night, but she had no idea whether it was one in the morning or five. Somewhere out in the dark, a siren wailed, but only for a short time, as though a night bird had given a few heart-rending cries, only to fall silent again. She thought about Edvin, and then she thought about all the people she would meet in the future, and even though she had no idea who they were or where they were, it was an uplifting thought.

When the doctor, a woman of about Lydia's age, finally appeared, she held an X-ray photograph in each hand. She held them up in front of the patient in a jovial manner, and Lydia listened attentively to what was said. It was good news. A slight concussion and a couple of fractured ribs, that was all. The doctor asked how Lydia felt. Lydia said she was pleased that everything had gone so well. She politely declined the offer of a hospital bed for the night. She wanted to get home. She longed to be alone. Any grief over her mother's death had somehow been suppressed by the volume of unnecessary details.

OLD FARMER'S
ALMANAC

When cattle sniff the air around midday, when they flare their nostrils and cavort with their tails in the air, expect bad weather.

When pigs gather straw in their mouths, it will soon rain; when pigs do not settle at night, rain can be expected the next day.

When frogs croak loudly or can be seen in greater numbers, it will soon rain.

When fleas, flies, and mosquitoes all swarm, expect rain and cloudy weather.

However, when midges dance in great numbers at dusk, fair weather can be expected the following day.

Likewise, a dry day can be expected when dung beetles fly in the evening.

When spiders are busy with their webs, a period of dry weather can be expected. But if they are lazy and drowsy, bad weather can be expected. And if they continue to work in the rain, it is only a short shower.

Ants and beetles prepare for a storm many hours before it hits.

If a dog eats grass, howls, and smells bad, it will soon rain.

Likewise, if a cat eats grass and sharpens its claws, rain can be expected.

When swallows fly so high in the evening that they can barely be seen in the sky, the next day is normally glorious. But if they fly so low that their wings brush the ground or water, it will rain before long.

When magpies build their nests high up in the tree, it will be a wet summer, but if they build their nest low, the summer will be fair.

If geese and ducks cluster together as they swim, rain can be expected.

If the grasshopper does not jump high, you can expect good weather, but when it does jump high, there will be rain and storms.

If the chaffinch can be heard before dawn, rain is on the way.

A bee outside the hive will never be surprised by rain.

When flocks of gulls fly inland and settle on the fields, a storm is brewing.

EVEN IN THE
WHITE NIGHTS

Lydia woke up very early, as always. For a moment, she was not quite sure where she was, but when she realized she was at home in her own bed, she was filled with contentment. She ran her hand over the bandage that had been pulled tight around her ribs, just under her breasts, with a strap over the one shoulder to hold it in place. Even though it was cold in the room, she had slept naked. No pain, just a slight tenderness. She pulled on a pair of pants and a T-shirt and went out into the living room to light the stove, and while she sat and waited for the wood to catch fire, she drank a cup of black coffee and ate a couple of oatcakes with butter and jam. Then she showered and got dressed as carefully as she could, before driving to the clinic. The unexpectedly mild weather had transformed the snow into slush. She turned the corner at the town hall and saw a young boy crossing the street. It was Johan. Lydia gave the horn a gentle tap to draw his attention. Johan stopped and looked at the car with distrust. He clearly did not recognize her. She rolled down the window and asked where he was going. He told her he had missed the bus. He was always too late, he said. Lydia leaned over the passenger seat, taking care not to stretch her muscles, pushed open the door, and told him to get in. She asked how the dog was. He answered by saying that his mother thought he made up all kinds of stuff. But it was his mother who made things up, he said. For example, she said he was allergic to dogs. But he wasn't allergic to that dog. He'd had it in his room for several days and everything was fine, but then he got a cold. He coughed at night and his mother heard him. She found the dog under his bed and said that was why he was ill, but he only had a cold. Where was the dog now? The boy looked away. The vet had put it down. Lydia pulled into the bus stop outside the school. She straightened his fringe and asked when he was finished for the day, and they agreed that she would come and collect him after his last class. She had no idea what she was doing, only that it was necessary, not to get attached to him in any way, it wasn't that, rather that she wanted to show him he could trust her. If there was no trust, what good was anything? Did she have her mother to thank for her confidence in this? She had no idea what to make of it. How could one know for sure where things like that came from? How could one know what was one's own? She thought she was one of those travellers who tended to forget the most important piece of luggage at home.

When she got to the clinic, she parked under the big maple trees. There was a mild breeze, but no rustling or movement in the treetops, all was silent. She got out, put her hands on the roof of the car, spread her fingers, and drew in the southerly wind. It was a peculiar way to grieve, she thought, just to carry on and hold on to everything so tight. She closed her eyes, she pictured the summer, an approaching summer with marigolds and poppies, and the scent of lavender from afar, her father was bathed in sunlight at home on the farm, there was the smell of dried fertilizer, the heat made the wooden panels groan, and the rebellious bees buzzed in the hives. Her father turned toward her, put a hand up to shadow his eyes. There was something gloomy and grave about him. He had a wretched demeanour. Even in the white nights, he wanted to be left in peace.

Lydia liked spending time at work. There was always something to study, something practical to think about: the medicine cabinets with matte glass doors, the solid work surfaces, the bottles of pills, the shining instruments. It felt good to be there with all the others, people with whom she shared her profession. It was an unpredictable and hectic world with no room for vague illusions, no time for idling, only delight and defeat in quick succession.

When Lydia came in the door, she bumped into Sigurd Brandt. He looked confused. He put a hand on her shoulder and shook his head but said nothing, it almost seemed that whatever it was he had on his mind absorbed him completely. They went together into his office, a large but sparsely furnished room with a worn desk in the middle, files stuffed with paper in the bookshelves, and a couple of cardboard boxes where he kept discarded equipment. Brandt sat down on the windowsill. Lydia observed him. He cleared his throat, then began to ask her about Johan, if she knew him well, if she had spoken to his mother. Lydia replied that she had only met him in connection with the dog and that she knew nothing about his parents. Brandt told her, outright, that his father was a loser who had left the mother and son years ago, and then said, again without further ado, that the mother was a spiteful and difficult woman. Lydia said she had spoken to Johan no more than half an hour ago, and Brandt asked if he had said anything about the dog. When she said that he had, he turned toward the window. He leaned his fists on the windowsill, stood there as though something outside had caught his attention, then told her that someone had found the dog at the garbage dump, that she, Johan's mother, had not even bothered to put it in a plastic bag. Despite the gravity of this news, Lydia felt a twinge of relief. Even though she was sure that no one at the clinic had put the animal down, as Johan thought, and told her, no doubt misled by his mother, it was good to have it confirmed. She saw the boy's anguished face in front of her and thought that his mother had shown a lack of insight that bordered on abhorrent. And then it struck her that she had now completely forgotten her own mother. She had forgotten Dagmar, who lay under the earth and was irrefutably erased. She gasped, it was impossible to hold it back. Brandt turned toward her but did not seem to notice what a frail state she was in. Ah well, Lydia. He hoped that she'd had a good holiday. Now it was time to get on. Lydia nodded and left the office. She went to the reception and talked to Bård, the trainee. He was the one who had an overview of the day's appointments. He gave her a yellow sticky note. Lydia had to go and see a sow. The farm was some distance away. She looked at her watch to check if she could still be back in time to pick Johan up from school. Just as the door was about to close behind her, she heard Bård calling. He wondered if he could go with her. He was finished for the day in any case. Lydia said he was more than welcome. In the car she asked if he would not rather go home, she could drop him off; after all, he had a free evening. But no, he wanted to use the time to learn the tricks of the trade, the ones you could not read up on.

It was a long drive to the high-lying farm, and the narrow road wound its way up through a stretch of dense forest. The road surface was buckled, with great tears. Oily gravel lay in the pot-holes and cracks. Even though it was daylight, it felt like driving through a dimly lit tunnel. Bård said very little, he sat humming to himself and looked out of the window, he seemed to be happy, not in a superficial or fleeting way. There was always something light and good-willed about him, Lydia had noted, and even though she had not had much to do with him, he was attentive and present whenever they passed on the way in and out of the clinic, or happened to meet by the coffee machine in the kitchen.

The farmer was waiting out in the muddy yard. He greeted them briefly and they followed him to the pigsty where the sow was lying, breathing heavily with a litter of piglets crawling around her. It was obvious that the animal was suffering. A boar lay on its belly, grunting, in the pen beside her. The farmer opened the gate. He kneeled down in front of the pig and patted her. He seemed awkward and hesitant. Why doesn't he say anything? Lydia wondered. And then, as though he had read Lydia's thoughts, Bård took her bag and went into the pen. He took the animal's temperature, then proceeded to examine the pig with the ambitious thoroughness of a novice.

He took his time before turning to the farmer and asking if he had needed to assist with the birth. The farmer confessed, in a mumble, that the birth had, as he guessed, not been straightforward. It had been necessary to assist. Bård stood up. He washed his hands with alcohol and waved them around until they were dry. It was metritis, he said. The farmer looked at Lydia, not with suspicion but rather a degree of reluctance. He asked if she was not going to examine the pig as well, but there was no need, she said. They gave the animal some pain-killers and antibiotics, and said that should do the trick.

On the way back, the weather changed. Damp gusts of wind hit the windshield, and a flash of lightning lit up the ridge of the hills. Lydia waited for the rumble of thunder, which was more like a short, dry cough when it eventually came. Bård mumbled something about how odd it was to have thunder at this time of year, and then, as if there was a connection, a red thread that only he could see, he asked if perhaps Lydia would like to have dinner with him one evening. He looked out the side window as he asked, as though what he had said, or the answer that would come, had nothing to do with him. Then he started to hum again. He was asking her out, and he was humming. Perhaps it was to underline that the suggestion was of a casual nature. Lydia cleared her throat, to ensure she had control of her voice, then she put all qualms to one side and said she would very much like to go out with him. He looked at her and smiled. She smiled back. Then they both turned their gaze forward, and neither said anything more until they were back at the clinic.

ON SUNDAY
SHE THOUGHT ABOUT
NOTHING AT ALL

D ecember arrived, and with December, the cold returned. Once again there was snow on the ground and tiny crystals danced in the biting air. You had to walk around with your eyes narrowed, because if you opened them wide, the quiet, vibrating winter light might dazzle you. Lydia spent much of her time with Johan in the days that followed. She picked him up after school and they went back to her house and had something to eat, or she would make sandwiches for them both and they would go skiing or sledding on one of the steeper slopes. Everything felt new to Lydia. She soon realized she was in the middle of something diffuse, their curious friendship was encircled by blurry edges, and this made her both open and giddy. Small everyday things were repeated in the boy's company, repeated quite simply because they were vital and inexhaustible, it was as though all the small things had linked together to become one great, everlasting experience.

Because of their busy shifts, Bård and Lydia had not yet managed to settle on a date to meet. It was hard to find an evening that suited them both. They had not seen much of each other since their visit to the pig farm. Bård spent much of his time in town, preparing for his exams, and whenever he was in the clinic, Lydia had the day off or was busy with Johan. But one Sunday, quite late in the evening, Bård rang her. He suggested they could go out the following Tuesday, when neither of them had a shift. Lydia said she would like that. She ended the conversation and lay back on the sofa. She closed her eyes. She was sitting onboard an airplane, and the plane rose up through the clouds, a few seconds later she saw the shadow of the aircraft on the white, billowy surface. She stood up and went to the bathroom. She brushed her teeth in the dark, sat down on the edge of the bath. Who is embarking on a journey? she thought. Mother, she said. No reply. Of course there was no reply. She thought about her father at home, abandoned and empty, not only empty, but hollow, because when one loses the person with whom one has shared a long life, one is hollowed out and cut off, and the loneliness blows straight through as he walked around there on the farm, there was no protection. Perhaps she should call him, talk to him, but what was the point? He offered neither confidences nor immediate confessions. If he needed her, he would have contacted her himself. Perhaps it was the desire to understand that bothered Lydia. When she was self-pitying, she might think it was her father's grim silence that restrained their curiosity, as such a silence contained a clear demand, it was a distraction that was, more than anything, akin to oblivion or negligence. As a teenager, Lydia had dreamed of having a boyfriend who appreciated her every move. But even though neither her father nor mother had said it outright, she soon learned that such dreams were petty, almost evil. One should strive to live a decent life, and a decent life was essentially synonymous with an unobtrusive life. But her father's own inadequacy, what was the significance of that? The fact that he tried to conquer a reality that constantly evaded him? Or did it bother him, the realization that an action, a defeat, or a moment of joy never unfolded as neatly as a calculation?

A GLIMMER

After the meal, Bård and Lydia took a taxi back to her house. They shared another bottle of wine, and then, despite Lydia's sore ribs, they made love with a rough urgency until they fell asleep. In the morning, a slight embarrassment hung between them, which was reinforced when Bård thanked her before he left, not only with a hug and kiss, but also with a polite handshake. She went back to bed, stretched out, and smiled to herself when she thought of his boyish retreat. What had happened was more unforeseen than intended. Their meeting had indeed been unrestrained, driven by lust even, but Lydia knew that, for her part, it was already a closed affair, and she was certain it would have no painful repercussions. They had treated each other with respect rather than tenderness, and that was how it would always be. She took a shower and got dressed. Bård had left his brown leather gloves behind. Lydia found them behind the shoe rack in the hall. She put them on the kitchen table. Johan would be coming soon. She had promised to take him up the hill to where the slopes were long and steep. Her night with Bård and the interrupted sleep had left her impatient. She went outside.

She waited in the rosy glow of dawn, and as she stood there without doing anything at all, she felt free of worries. It was as baffling as it might be if a letter were to disappear from the alphabet. Johan came by bus. He struggled to get his toboggan out the back door but was helped by a girl, who he forgot to thank, and was a bit perplexed maybe, Lydia thought; at that age it was so easy to feel embarrassed and clumsy in situations like that, as though the other people were suddenly part of your dreams. Lydia went to meet him. Was he hungry? It was always sensible to have some food before spending a long day in the snow. And sure enough, he had not eaten. He hadn't had time, he said. What with one thing and another. Lydia cut some slices of bread and made two peanut butter sandwiches, and two with ham and thin slices of cucumber. Did Johan know that the doubling up of two slices was invented by someone called John Montagu, the 4th Earl of Sandwich? Did he know that the town Sandwich was not far from Canterbury, where the Archbishop Thomas Becket was killed in his own cathedral by four knights? Goodness, why all this information? Now they needed to get up to the slopes, while the slopes still had some sun on them.

They sledded and played in the snow until dusk started to fall. Johan seemed to be enjoying himself, but then he began to flail around with the blue toboggan, which he dragged behind him on a far-too-short rope. Lydia stopped to wait for him, and when he caught up with her, she asked if he was sad. And instead of answering, he asked if she'd had a visitor. Lydia squinted at him. She suggested that she should drive him home. The sun was about to go down, and they were both cold. She took the toboggan and they started walking toward the car. Johan now chatted happily away. He thought maybe he had caught a cold, and then he revealed that when he had been in the house, he had seen some gloves on the kitchen table. They weren't hers, were they? Lydia put their stuff into the trunk and they got in the car. They were both quiet on the way home. When Lydia stopped in front of the house where Johan lived, the boy turned to her and thanked her. He'd had a lovely afternoon. Maybe they could meet again soon. Lydia told him to have something warm to drink. She watched his skinny, stooped silhouette as he jogged through the snow. The outside light by the front door came on, and moments later a woman appeared in the doorway. Lydia wished that Johan would turn round, just for a second. Not once had they mentioned the dog or his mother's fatal actions. But then, when they were feeling close, Johan had asked her a deeply personal question. Was there a hint of reproach in his voice? No, no, she was sure there was no reproach, just the careless curiosity of a young person.

THE ROCKET MAN

Lydia worked through Christmas. She only had the twenty-seventh off, and then asked Johan if he wanted to come over. They watched cartoons together and he had his PlayStation with him, which he plugged into the television so he could show her the games he had been given. She spent the final few hours of the year with Bård, who came to her house when his shift ended, which had seemed endless, apparently. They drank and made love. Lydia enjoyed the company, but the whole affair reminded her more of the loose arrangements from her student years than of a burgeoning relationship. She had some days off immediately after New Year and took the opportunity to drive north to visit her father. Lydia had phoned and agreed to this with him, and he sounded pleased that his daughter was coming to visit. But when she got there, everything was as before. He was standing by the outhouse, pouring something that resembled left-over chicken soup onto the snow and barely lifted his head when she drove up. She gave him a self-conscious hug and then went in. The house smelled of food and dust, newspapers that were weeks old lay helter-skelter on the chairs, and the mantelpiece was covered in soot and grease. There was no hint of any recent Christmas celebrations. Lydia chose not to comment on the neglect. Instead she started to tidy. Her father watched. The table was far too big when Dagmar was no longer there, he said.

Lydia did the washing up. She put the clean glasses and plates back in the cupboard and the cutlery back in the drawer, then rinsed her hands. Her father spoke in short bursts; being alone left one open to the strangest thoughts—spiritualists, for example, who claim they can talk to dead; one almost hoped they were telling the truth. Lydia stroked his head. He needed a haircut. She told him she could tidy up his hair so he would not need to bother about it. And less than half an hour later, when she gently lifted the towel from his shoulders and brushed away any hairs from his neck, she thought his distance was more idiotic than hurtful. She told him she was finished, and he got up and left the bathroom without a word, left the kitchen chair where it was, as though it was not his job to tidy up, as though nothing was his responsibility any longer. She washed his hair down the sink, it was too thin to cause a blockage. She knew it was vital not lose her humour. Any attempts to engage on her part had to be seen as friendly. An argument or confrontation would not win any favours with the old man. She went into the living room to see if he was there. There were some dull thumps from upstairs. He had clearly gone to bed.

Lydia picked the key up from the turquoise enamel dish on the sideboard, put it in the lock, and turned it resolutely. How many years had she resisted doing this? Now everything that was secret was going to be revealed. She did not hesitate. She would have broken the lock if necessary. She would have found a big screwdriver or some other suitable tool and prised open the door, and the dark wood would have been damaged forever. But the key did what a key should do, and the door opened as smoothly as it would if the hinges had just been oiled. There was nothing mysterious or of any note in the cupboard. Carefully folded tablecloths and other linen lay stacked on the top shelf, and on the bottom shelf sat a large cardboard box full of old Christmas decorations, and a smaller box, with a lid tied up with string. She carried this out into the kitchen. No letters, no diaries, not even a few short lines on a postcard or a couple of forgotten notes—only old brochures advertising agricultural machinery and feed concentrates, pamphlets from the medical centre and a folded film poster. It was as though her parents had, with the caution of foresight, weeded out anything that might give away something private. Lydia opened up the poster with care. The once glossy but now dull paper was spry and reluctant. The actors were listed in the top right-hand corner. The illustration was in black and white, with a bold yellow brush stroke to give the impression of speed and movement. It was of a flying robot with its hands held out and up above its head. Or was it an astronaut? Under him, a city was crumbling. *King of the Rocket Men*, it said. "A different film, packed with dynamite action. See Jeff King's fantastic battle with the mad Dr. Vulcan—the world's most dangerous evil genius." Underneath, in the right-hand corner: "Distribution Svea Film Stockholm" and a small logo, and then at the very bottom, in tiny letters that were difficult to read in the half-light: "Borås Kliché & Litografiska AB." For many reasons, it felt important to study even the smallest detail, as there might be a secret hidden away all the same. It was like discovering an old chest without any obvious locking mechanism and then trying to find the small button, the hidden pressure point that would flip open the lock. She sat there looking through the papers and reading. It was a pointless exercise, and when she finally realized that it was the disappointment of having found nothing of value that had led her on such a wild goose chase, she regretted that she had even fallen for the temptation to open the cupboard. And she was tired and stiff after the long drive. She put the meagre pickings back in the box and put the box back on the shelf.

The next morning, her father woke her with breakfast in bed. He had brewed some strong black coffee, spread a thick layer of butter on a couple of slices of bread, and filled a small, sticky bowl with honey. He put the tray down on the chair that served as a bedside table, gently shook his daughter awake, and said that it was a bitterly cold day outside. Lydia watched as he padded out of the room. She thought that it was not so much common sense that he lacked, he lacked lightness. The door closed with a bang, and soon after, as she ate her breakfast, Lydia heard the tractor outside.

At suppertime, it was Lydia's turn to offer a meal. She had driven to the shop and bought what was needed, and although it was nothing fancy, she had made a good and simple dish with boiled potatoes and wild salmon stuffed with herbs and vegetables, which she then wrapped in tin foil and baked in the oven. She found a bottle of aquavit in one of the kitchen cupboards that she poured into a couple of small dram glasses that stood shining on the white tablecloth. She thought that sitting down at a table, getting a little tipsy, and eating a meal was one of the greatest pleasures one could share with others. She raised her glass, and her father did the same. They drank it down in one go and then tucked into the fish. Johan said they should have set a place for Dagmar too, as a gesture now that they were together again. Lydia did as he said. She got out a third plate, cutlery, and a glass, which she filled. And there they sat, father and daughter, they refilled their glasses and raised them. Alcohol helps when there's not much to say to each other, Lydia thought. She felt the alcohol course through her body, a warm movement that softened all tension. She looked over at her father. His eyes had always been shinier than her mother's, as they were moister. He may well have noticed that his daughter was studying him, but he did not let it bother him. He helped himself to two healthy portions of food. Only once did he say that the food was good. When he finally pushed his plate to one side, he gave his daughter a compliment, and it seemed every bit as hasty as when he had slammed the door shut that morning. He said she was beautiful. Just that: You are beautiful, Lydia. Then he said nothing more, as though he lacked the words. Lydia felt the blood rush to her cheeks. She stood up and cleared the table. Out in the kitchen, she was struck by a peculiar dizziness. It was unlike her to drink so much. She let the tap run, leaned forward, and drank the cold water, but it only made things worse. She excused herself, said she wasn't feeling well. Her father nodded. He sat down on the sofa and turned on the television. Lydia felt herself blanch on the stairs, a cold sweat broke out on her forehead, even the otherwise comforting creaks on the steps were now grating, almost painful. Annoyed at her pitiful state, Lydia lay down on her stomach in bed. She remained there, floating. The room's simple furnishings were reminiscent of a boat with hard benches and waterlogged floorboards. Lydia could feel it rocking. She registered that her father came into the room to check on her. Did he speak to her? It didn't really matter. She didn't have the strength to answer. She allowed herself to be lifted into sleep by the gentle waves.

When she woke up the next morning, she found a glass of cloudy homemade apple juice on the chair. She reluctantly sat up and drank the juice in one go. The sun was shining outside. She decided to go and see her mother's grave. It was like saying: Let's move on. Half an hour later, at the cemetery, which was of the plain sort, a piece of ground given to the dead in a bygone age, she was delighted to find paw prints in the snow around the graves. Her father had put out a lantern, but the wick in the candle was still white and untouched. He must have forgotten to light it, or perhaps he had come here in daylight and thought there was no point leaving the flame flickering in the sun. The small wooden church cast a sharp shadow over the cemetery, and even though it looked as if it was no longer used—the paint was peeling off the eastern wall, and two of the windowpanes had been replaced with insulation mats—it still inspired confidence. It stood there, on guard and alive somehow, and everything around it was out of danger. Lydia folded her hands and prayed that her mother had finally found peace, and as soon as she had whispered this innocent request, she heard a car stop on the road. She turned around and shaded her eyes. A person got out. It was Eivor. Lydia walked to meet her. She soon saw that the woman was wearing far-too-thin clothes, and she asked if anything was wrong. Eivor apologized for interrupting, but she was in a desperate situation. One of the horses on her farm had injured itself and it would take the vet ages to get there. Lydia indicated that she should get in the car. She checked the bag of equipment she always kept in the trunk. Eivor showed her the way. The horse had fallen through the ice, she said. Luckily the water was not too deep and there was no real current there. She and her husband had got help from the neighbours. They had had to chop down a tree to get out to the open channel. They had tied a rope around the horse's neck and that way managed to get it up onto land. But it had taken some time, and the animal was suffering from hypothermia.

The poor beast was lying in the stable, shivering and snorting under a mountain of sheepskins and rugs. Eivor's husband shook Lydia's hand and thanked her for coming. Lydia squatted down and pulled away everything that was covering the horse's body. It was as though she were preparing to perform a magic trick. She checked its heartbeat, opened its closed eyes, and the light floated up in them. She ran her hands all over the strong animal's rough coat. It was as if everything in the great body had locked, joints and sinews and muscles all jammed. Slowly, and with great care, the three of them managed to get the horse to stand up. It neighed and kicked the air, broke free, and leapt erratically out into the yard. It really was a magic trick. And Lydia stood there, uncertain of how it had happened. A bit like an equation where one arrives at the correct answer without being able to explain quite how one got that result. Eivor and her husband praised Lydia's purpose and energy. They invited her to dinner, but she politely refused. When she was a child, she said and pointed, when she was a girl, she used to climb the closest peaks in order to swim in one of the lakes on the other side. The water there was warm in the summer.

Back at the farm, Johan had been told about what had happened. It was Eivor who had phoned him to praise Lydia's work, and she had laid it on pretty thick. Johan was impressed and more than a little proud, and he expressed this new-found respect by shaking his daughter's hand, and he nodded as he said: Well, I'll be damned, you're good.

The next morning, Lydia said goodbye. She hugged her father. The thin, sinewy man seemed to carry a tiredness that Lydia thought was symptomatic of the fact that there was no longer anyone to wait for. She asked if he wanted to come with her, so he could see for himself how she lived in Norway, but he declined. She walked toward the car, stopped, looked back. He had not moved. But then he lifted both his arms and stroked back his hair. It almost seemed that he wanted to draw attention to his hands, which were still strong and agile.

WHAT SHE
COULD IMAGINE

Spring came early. Milder winds blew in at the start of March, and the melting snow dripped and ran down the gutters and pipes. Was it just a false promise? No, the warmth continued, the grass swelled and released its scent, the treetops filled out and lifted their heads, and what had been sparse and insignificant now became vital and intensely present. Her self-esteem grew too, and even though Lydia had broken off with Bård when he finished his placement and moved north, her days were more appeasing, her nights hopeful. She carried out her work with a kind of unrestrained equilibrium, the light served her well, and even in the middle of a critical situation with blood and shit up to her elbows, she heard the gentle twittering outside in the sunshine. She was where she wanted to be, in the country, in the provinces. She found herself thinking that this paradoxical existence, the lethargic and good-natured satisfaction that came with spring, had been bestowed on her. She occupied herself with leisurely activities at home. She studied various anatomy books, made notes about the day's events in her light blue journal, brief outlines, the odd question, this and that to look up, things she wanted to explore more. But most of all, she liked to work on the herb bed. She got immense pleasure from this sheltered corner of the garden and the small piece of ground she was constantly expanding. Even at sunset there was light enough, and she would carry on digging, weeding, and raking until darkness fell. There was a beautiful slowness to these chores. And the lush miniature landscape was teeming with tiny creatures that wriggled and crept peacefully around or fled in terror from the giant being's hands.

THE WOMAN
FROM ANTWERP

Lydia could no long remember the origins of the sentence she had scribbled down: "Fear is an essential instinct, and this instinct is linked to a grey, almond-shaped mass deep in the brain." It was her own formulation, that she did remember, based on what she had read, an interpretation, in other words, an understanding, and now there it was, in between her notes from last spring's lambing season and a short remark about her mother, and it said nothing about what she had thought or in which context she had written it down. Beside it, it said: "It is best to remain silent in anger or grief," and this phrase too had something enigmatic about it. She put the book back in the desk drawer and looked over at Johan, who was sitting at the dining table doing his homework. His unruly hair shone copper in the light from the window. It was obvious that he was struggling. He chewed on his pencil, and his eyes were glazed and distant as they so often were when faced with complex tasks. Lydia asked if he needed help. He looked over at her and shrugged. She took that as a yes.

When he had finished his homework, Johan went with her to check on a cow at one of the farms high up on the hillside above the defunct cellulose factory. They drove along the river, past the old wooden buildings with gardens that almost toppled over into the turbulent water. Now, with the spring thaw, the water was muddy and brown. The sunlight vanished when they turned into a forested area, but as soon as they emerged onto the gentle hillside, it flooded over them again. The trees stood fluttering their iridescent green crowns, and the pollen sparkled in the breeze. Johan asked if she knew what was wrong with the cow, but Lydia could only repeat what the farmer had told her. It would not eat and had been unwell for more than a week. Johan rolled down the side window, his hair blew back, and he closed his eyes. It was his mother who had killed the dog, he said, out of the blue. Lydia noticed that she immediately steeled herself. It was pure instinct, in the way one protects oneself when assailed. And Johan had more on his mind: he knew when she wasn't telling the truth, he said, because she always looked away and busied herself with something, something unimportant: folding the laundry, emptying the dishwasher. Johan leaned back in the seat and rolled up the window again. But Lydia had mended the dog, he said. It had been as good as new. Lydia, for her part, had no well-formulated phrases or any comfort to offer, but she wanted to give him the acknowledgement he deserved, so she nodded. But now the boy was almost frantic; his mother had said that it wasn't natural that he spent so much time with her. Lydia felt the shock run through her. Johan sat there, so distressed, his head to one side, his face turned away from her. She parked the car in the shade of the mature copper beach tree that was planted in front of the farmhouse. The woman who came out to meet them was not much older than Lydia. She spoke with an accent. She was slim and attractive, but when Lydia took her hand, she felt the strength in her grip. The woman pointed toward the barn with a nervous movement and then led them across the dusty yard. Lydia started to examine the animal. Johan watched with interest. He was almost in her way as she moved round the poor, weak creature. She tried to open the cow's mouth, and the reaction was immediate, it pulled back its head, rolled its eyes, and started to bellow alarmingly. The woman moved closer, put her arm over the animal's broad back, and managed to calm it down. Lydia pressed a syringe into its jaw, pushed the needle through into the gum, and as soon as the anaesthetic started to take effect, she managed to prise open its stubborn mouth. She inserted a piece of wood to ensure that it would not snap shut on her fingers. The back of the mouth cavity was swollen and full of clumps of coagulated blood. Lydia poured water from a bucket into the cow's badly mutilated mouth. Red water splashed out onto the floor. She waved Johan and the woman over. A bent nail had ripped open one side of the tongue and become embedded in the palate. Lydia put her hands into the mouth and pulled out the infernal thing. Fresh blood oozed out. She felt the edges of the wound to establish what kind of suture was needed. She got out the antibiotics, took the time to wink to Johan, who was standing there with his mouth open too. There was an honest contentment to her every action. She was tense, but nothing in what she said or did would draw attention to anything other than certitude and determination.

Out in the sun, when the work had been done, Lydia commented on the old copper beech. It was exquisite. Exquisite. A word she had never used before. The foreign lady made her feel confused in an unexpected way. What was her name? Lydia had typically not caught her name. And where was she from? A port city. From Antwerp. She had wanted to make a fresh start and had always dreamed of living in a country with high mountains. Lydia and Johan were invited into the house. Johan asked if he could keep the nail. He held it up like a small trophy.

When they stepped inside the house, Lydia was surprised by a sense of well-being. There was something impeccable about the way in which the Belgian woman spoke and behaved. A friendly remark, a generous smile. The more one sees of men, Lydia thought, the more tempting it is to say that they are all alike, in daily life at least, in the way they speak. There was possibly no deeper truth to this observation, Lydia recognized that, but now she was sitting at a kitchen table that had been painted a bold red, and everything felt so extraordinarily real: the bread, the crispy crust that broke as soon as it was pulled, the crumbs that showered down onto the plates and surrounding table—all the small, wholesome details. And the conversation, even though it seemed to dry up now and then, was still free and liberating. She felt so responsive, so amenable. It was like saying: Don't you want to join me in the way that I join you?

The same evening, when she was finally alone, Lydia lay outside in the hammock. Her lips felt swollen in the warm, dry wind that playfully caressed the garden. As she dozed, she imagined that everything around her smelled of bread and caraway. She conjured up an image of the woman from Antwerp, enjoyed seeing her again. She leaned forward, rested her cheek on the red table. What was it she said she was called? Lise. It was Lise, wasn't it? But could that really be the case? No Belgian woman is called Lise, surely. Nathalie and Danielle, Marguerite perhaps, but what were the chances of Lise being used in northern Flanders? Did she live with her husband? No, she lived alone. She was not married, had never attached herself to anyone in that way. A tractor hurried past on the old road. The dust was blown away by the strengthening wind. Lydia dried the spittle from the corners of her mouth, swung her feet round and down onto the grass. She walked drowsily into the house, switched off the few lights that were on. The ceiling light in the hall, the one over the table in the dining room. There were no curtains in the house, only blinds on the windows that faced the road.

Lydia had just slipped down under the duvet when the telephone rang. It was her father. Not that he had anything particular on his mind, he just wanted to know how she was. Lydia heard that he was coughing. He asked if she could remember the time he found her under the raised-floor storehouse. How old was she then? Four or five? Lydia did not recall the occasion he was talking about. Oh, could she not remember that she used to crawl around under the storehouse, and when he asked her what she was looking for, she said she was looking for an animal she could feed? Even a carousel horse, her father said, could awaken her soft-hearted instincts. Lydia told him she could not remember. And what was more, there was nothing soft-hearted or self-sacrificing about her relationship with animals. It was the fact that the work was so tangible and practical that appealed to her. Her mother had once said one should strive to keep things alive, and she used the word *things*, that identifiable and practical concept that can be used when one wants to embrace all forms of life in the world. And the expression *one must strive*, in her mother's vocabulary, was synonymous with integrity.

Lydia asked if her father wanted to come and visit her. Her father hesitated, coughed again. Was he ill? That didn't sound very good. No, no, he wasn't ill. He was never ill. He just had the shivers. It would pass soon enough. And, well, it was a long way to drive. Lydia said he could take the train. He could leave the car in Trondheim and take the train from there. But no, trains were not really his thing. He had never got used to the railways. All the people. And no smoking carriage any longer either. There was a pause. Then he said he needed freedom. He had to have free hands. Lydia had no idea what he meant. She was about to ask him to explain, but he beat her to it: he could not promise anything, he could not say exactly when, but he would make the journey one day.

ONE DAY SHE HEARD
HERSELF TALKING

igurd Brandt treated Lydia as one would a friend, with care and respect. It was well-known that the vet appreciated his colleague's independence and reliability. Lydia thought he saw himself in her, and that his acknowledgement of her in many ways was a reflection of his own recognition in the community. For long periods they were both so busy that they were unable to talk, but whenever they did meet, Brandt offered her kind words. Now and then his praise was so general that she suspected his approval was simply encouragement. But that was how Brandt was—as fleeting as he was friendly and generous. They only did one job together that spring. It was a routine job, but they were both needed as they were going to vaccinate the sheep on one of the big farms. They drove there in Brandt's car, and Brandt was in fine form. It seemed he was using the opportunity to update himself. One question followed another, and Lydia answered as best she could. How were Lydia's parents? Lydia told him her mother had passed away in the winter, but, all things considered, her father was doing well. Brandt looked at her. How little he knew about her, he said. Did she cut oranges in half or peel them, and did she separate each segment? And had she found herself a man yet? No, there wasn't really time for that, Lydia replied, noticing how absurd this little statement sounded. And Brandt had heard that she was looking out for Johan. That was worthy of respect. Lydia simply shrugged. In a fit of irrational confidentiality, she might have told him more about the quiet life she led, about the days with Johan, about her father, about the loss of her mother, and, well, she might even have told him about Bård. Brandt would no doubt have understood. But what was the point? What would such openness inspire?

Brandt asked if she remembered Edvin. Edvin, whom she met at the dinner party last year? He had gone through a difficult divorce, and his wife had tried to take her own life, or threatened to do so. Lydia listened attentively, filled with relief. After all, it was action, not speculation, that counted. What a fool she had been. She who had believed Edvin was a lost cause, someone to be forgotten. She could not help but smile, and she noticed that Brandt noticed but made no comment. He clearly did not want to know any unnecessary details. Lydia registered that he had lost weight. His eyes were just as piercing and inquisitive as before, but she noted that there was something more pensive about him.

The work was done over the course of two days, and when they had finished and were driving home, Brandt stopped at a gas station. He wanted to treat Lydia to an ice cream. They sat down in the sun. Edvin had asked after her, Brandt said as he enjoyed his ice cream with such abandon that the chocolate casing broke into pieces that fell into his lap. He flicked them away. When there was no response from Lydia, he asked her if she found that strange. Strange? No, she didn't think it was strange. She listened attentively for more information or an explanation, but none came. Brandt stood up. It was obvious that he realized this was not the right time to talk of budding affairs and vague possibilities. Lydia pointed at his collar, to draw his attention to some melting ice cream. Brandt rubbed it away with his thumb.

When Lydia got home, Johan was lying in the hammock. He lay with his hands on his stomach and one leg dangling over the edge. If only he had been her own boy. The thought surprised her. And she seemed to freeze in the shade of the trees.

NO MAGICAL JOURNEYS,
NO GREAT DISCOVERIES OR
HEROIC ACHIEVEMENTS

I t was seldom that Lydia stayed in bed once she had woken up. As a rule, there was no option but to throw the duvet to one side as soon as the alarm clock rang and walk barefoot into the bathroom to splash cold water on her face. When she thought about it, it had been like that ever since she was a child. She wanted to get up and out into the new day, regardless of whether it was pleasures or duties that called. But now she had two weeks' holiday, two summer weeks, July days to fill as she pleased, and she chose to stay where she was. Not even the two wasps buzzing around the room got her out of bed. She reached for the notebook that lay on the floor beside the old apothecary's bottle filled with water. Before falling asleep, she had scribbled down some random sentences; they were about the boy, Johan, and the conflicting feelings that had surfaced so unexpectedly. She had simply felt compelled to write them down in plain text: Did she really want children? There seemed to be two loosely interwoven fates in the one single consideration. She thought of her own mother. There was a unique connection in their relationship too. She only had to hold up her hands, and even there in the half-light she would be able to trace her ancestry, the continuation. The long, sinewy fingers, white cuticles. The grey coat hung in the cupboard under the stairs, recently dry cleaned, as it was too warm to use it now in summer. In another time, in another era, her mother had worn it with pride. She had no doubt fallen for the elegant cut and the matte sheen of the woollen fabric. She had bought it in Stockholm. She went there on her own a couple of times a year. Not a very appealing thought, in Lydia's opinion. Her father was always a disappointment whenever Dagmar wanted to get away. If only a day trip, or a night in a cheap guesthouse. No, Johan had other things to do. There was always something to tinker with on the tractor, or he had to fix the roof on the outhouse, or it was hunting season. He was stubborn and often indignant on those occasions when he felt forced to defend his irregular and demanding work. And, to disguise his reactionary views, he used concepts such as "close to nature" and "upholding traditions," and thus justified continuing to live in a past age. Lydia shuddered to think about these onerous tasks. Even out of season, her father could sit for hours, indeed a full day, cleaning and polishing his old hunting rifle, and load it with cartridges, but he could not spare the time to leave the farm to keep his wife company for a couple of days in Stockholm or even just over in Sundsvall, because then the place might fall apart. On one of the trips south, her mother bought an electric coffee grinder. And that made Johan beam with joy, it was the first time Lydia heard him hum. Every morning he poured in the beans and sung softly to himself as the machine whirred and ground. He liked to pop a bean into his mouth and clearly relished the round, burnt taste. After a couple of years of steady use, the machine broke. Johan tried to fix it, but to no avail, it was not made to be repaired, and that decided the matter—he was not willing to buy a new one, they would just have to make do with ready-ground from the shop now, it never did anyone any harm.

Lydia would have loved to keep fresh flowers on her mother's grave. She envisaged herself standing by the entrance to the graveyard in the pollen-filled air, with a small daughter or son. What would she tell them? That her mother had been very beautiful when she was young, with chestnut hair, high cheekbones, and almond-shaped eyes? That she lost her cheerful and comforting disposition when Lydia was a teenager, and she seemed to wither away in the last years of her life?

While she brushed her teeth, Lydia studied her face in the mirror. There was nothing remarkable about the familiar features. She was not able to make up her mind whether she was beautiful or rather ordinary, not that it really mattered, she was happy with her quirks and qualities, and her body was toned and muscular in a feminine way, with a soft roundness over the shoulders and hips.

She lifted the water to her mouth to rinse out the toothpaste. She had no reason whatsoever to take a dim view of herself because she was single and childless, there was nothing lamentable or imposed about it. She had only recently turned thirty. She was who she was and lived as best she could. She had never been ill, had never suffered any stress, and had little experience of unhappy love. Was that not ample reason to feel grateful, even blessed? She shook her head at her own thoughts. Her work as a vet had taught her to see the smallest detail in everything. This sometimes resulted in a busyness that verged on the ridiculous.

From the upstairs window, she saw Johan down by the gate. He lifted his head when she called his name, looking around in bewilderment until he spotted her. Lydia told him the door was open and he could just come in. He seemed upset, gripped her hand as though it was a nervous first meeting. He was going to move, he told her. His mother had got a job somewhere in the northwest. And as he spoke, Lydia started to fold the laundry. The wind-dried clothes smelled faintly of flowers, grass. She listened to the boy's voice. When the last garment had been put away in the cupboard, she put her hand on his neck and asked if he was hungry, if he wanted to go swimming, if they should perhaps relax in the garden with their books. Three questions fired off in a row, almost on top of each other: impatient, restless.

They spent the afternoon by the sea. Johan swam back and forth between the rocks where Lydia lay sunbathing and a jetty that was some way out. He did this for more than half an hour before he got out. Then he dropped down beside her, took a deep breath, and sat there shivering, despite the heat. Lydia handed him a towel. He gave his hair a quick dry and pulled his T-shirt on over his head. He asked her if she dreaded him moving away. Lydia was not quite sure what to answer. Was that how he saw it? Was *he* worried about *her*? There was something odd about this radical change in roles. It was so unexpected, and

Johan's voice, which usually was irregular and full of stops and starts, now flowed calmly with a tenderness Lydia had not heard before. She felt unhelpful, just sitting there. She could not counter by saying that if he was happy, then she was happy too; he might interpret that as a rejection. Isn't it strange, Johan said, that when you fall in love, you sleep well at night, but you lose your appetite. Lydia asked if he had met a girl. And sure enough, he told her he had been exchanging emails with someone called Tine. Tine was the daughter of one of his mother's old school friends, she was his age and lived in the place they were moving to. He looked forward to meeting her. She was the only person he knew of who could hear a bat chirping. Hear a bat chirping? Yes, she could hear a bat's squeak. But how did he know that she could hear a bat chirping? Because she had told him. Lydia ruffled his hair. A motorboat passed below the rock. Lydia thought something incomprehensible had been avoided; only a few minutes before she had been tempted to say that he could stay with her. She had room enough. And who doesn't love a south-facing room that looks out onto the garden?

On the way up the scorched slope that led to where the car was parked, Johan spoke without interruption about the girl. Apparently they were both interested in the same things. She liked animals, dogs in particular, she collected stones, and she read Japanese comics. He only stopped talking when they got into the car, and as they drove, Lydia registered that he kept glancing over at her, but she pretended not to notice.

Before they went their separate ways, they agreed to meet and perhaps go to the cinema. They gave each other a hug, which was a bit awkward, because of the car seats. Johan held on to her hard and would not let go. It was as though he was reluctant or did not want to break a bond. When he did finally get out of the car, Lydia felt uneasy. Had she overlooked something important? She did not start the car until Johan had gone into the house, then she drove to the clinic, even though she knew she would not find the answer there. She knocked on Brandt's door, but there was no response. She tried the door, and it was unlocked. The light flashed on a stand of empty test tubes on the desk, where all kinds of equipment lay strewn—paraffin lamps, tweezers, a number of brown pill jars, a neurologist's hammer. There was something disheartening about the abandoned objects. Lydia went over to the window and looked out through a gap in the blinds. Outside, the white facade of the public swimming pool baked in the summer light, a van reversed up onto the pavement, the traffic lights by the pedestrian crossing changed from red to green without anyone crossing the street. Lydia felt dizzy. She grabbed hold of the office chair and sat down. She saw images. She was standing in the garden at home, and the grass had grown tall. Had she really let it grow so wild? She led a grey workhorse out into a cobbled square, and with a determined thrust of her hand pushed the bolt pistol straight into its forehead. The animal opened its eye wide in fright, and its tongue flapped in its snapping jaws. She was suddenly appalled by her own work: so many lives taken, so many hopeless cases; a dog with throat cancer, a sheep with advanced mastitis, a cow with gangrene in her udder. What could one do other than put an end to the suffering? After a while, Lydia managed to get up from the chair and stumbled over to the door. She quietly made her way out of the building, and when she emerged into the sunlight, Brandt drove up. He wound down the driver's window and asked if she was free on Saturday. They had invited Edvin for dinner and he had asked after her. They would all be delighted if she could come. Brandt offered this invitation without taking his eyes from her. Was it to see if there was any reaction? Lydia said she had no plans for the weekend, and she would very much like to come.

As soon as she got home, she took off her clothes, stepped out of her trousers, and her panties too, which fell from her knees and landed on the floor in a pink figure eight, like something she might have made in the handwork classes at school. She imagined the whole thing backwards with creative detail: the suppleness with which her panties slipped up her thighs, over all the bruises, and settled on her buttocks. She went into the bathroom without bothering to turn on the light, brushed her teeth, hard. She dreamed frequently, but her dreams did not tell her much. They were never about things like meeting a man or having children or reconciliation. They were unclear events and snippets, or that was certainly how she remembered them: an otter gnawing on an eel, an infinitely deep pool, a crystalline powder settling on her hands.

She shivered as she crept under the duvet. Even though it was probably nothing more than a summer flu, she was overwhelmed by the wish that someone was with her. She knew perfectly well that loneliness was not necessarily an evil.

Twosomeness was not always based on love, and what would such a connection actually give her? But the thought that she was going to meet Edvin again was uplifting all the same, and when Saturday came around, she woke up filled with a kind of suppressed anticipation, suppressed because all the assumptions she had made about Edvin seemed so fragile, so easy to tear to pieces. Was the whole thing a figment of her imagination? No, it was more that something had been set in motion without her really knowing what it would entail. Like a cool breeze in the heat, a mistaken season. She packed her swimming things in a bag and went to the coast, to her usual place. She swam a few lengths out to the raft. Feeling the strength of her body was pleasing. And after this invigorating session, she drove home.

She picked loose a lump of rosin from one of the trees in the garden, rubbed it between her thumb and index finger, drank in the smell. She looked around. The rhubarb had shot up into willing stalks, red as never before, the gooseberries had a matte sheen and in a few weeks would be bursting and ripe for picking.

It had been a while since she spoke to her father, she felt she should have been less confused when speaking to him. The spiritual distance was constant, and she had grown accustomed to it long ago, but now there was also time, months without a word that separated them, and Lydia wondered if she was perhaps too mean. Once when she was a girl, he had set the table out on the grass, and carried out large porcelain dishes of meatballs and pickled herring salad and strawberries and red radishes. A simple picture, and the words of a lullaby.

Outside the summer wind blows,
The cuckoo cries high in the linden tree.
Mother walks in the green meadow,
Lays her babe on a bed of flowers,
Scatters long trails
Of rose petals.

A kind of maturation process lay in these memories. With their cloying intensity they teased out a childish tendency: a need not to see things for what, in reality, they were, in the same way that a small porcelain figurine of the Virgin Mary and child can charm a poor soul.

THE CREATED

"From the hill, where the unassuming yet ancient and inviting church stood, embraced by the graveyard's leafy old trees, one has an overview of almost the entirety of the small parish, which unfolds its bounteous fields…offering a pleasing mix of vales and hills, the latter usually covered by deciduous or pine forests, but often cultivated and stone-free…Here, one does not speak of westerly winds, but rather westerly storms; west is the cardinal direction from whence the wind whines loudest…Then Sunday comes and is devoted to rest. We have reached the middle of August, and the farmer can, with a clear conscience, take a longer Sunday-afternoon nap than is his wont. He can snooze safe in the knowledge that the busiest time of year will soon be over and has been good. It has been an ideal summer. And even though the harvest month is little more than halfway through, the hay and autumn grains, the rye and the wheat, have already been taken in. Only the oats and root vegetables remain. There has not been such a bountiful harvest in living memory. The summer heat came as early as May, and when the spring floods subsided, the sun coaxed the shoots up, strong and rich, from the damp, steaming earth. And at pleasingly regular intervals, sunny days alternated with days and nights when the sky refreshed the soil with the necessary precipitation. It can, of course, never rain enough before midsummer. This year it was suitably moderate, truly the most desirable weather. After a cooling day of rain came a fresh wind, which set in motion the grass on the slopes and the tightly planted rye and wheat in the fields, so they became strong and resilient and could proudly hold their eager ears up to the sun. Then the blossom came, and neither torrential rain nor hail storms disturbed the flowering branches; instead the sun shone and gentle winds spread the pollen for fruiting. Not long after midsummer, the hay meadows were ready to cut, and the mowers clanked and creaked, whirring like giant crickets in competition with the corn crakes, while the scythes sang along the sides of the ditches, and flowers and ears fell to the sharp blades. Horse-drawn hay rakes and hand rakes gathered the sweet-smelling grass into great mounds that resembled the defences that warring armies of dwarves and dryads might build for their pretend battles. Then men and women with pitchforks and rakes came and gathered the mounds into haystacks or used their tools to help lift the grass onto newly constructed drying racks, which ran diagonally from northeast to southwest across the fields. The sun was scorching, but the work was a joy. Is there any work more delightful than haymaking in fine weather?"

THE COUNTRYSIDE
IN SUMMER

Out in the yard, Lydia looked down at her work clothes. Shit and blood on her thighs, her boots covered in muck. She was used to it, it was part of the job, but now she was aware of her appearance. Edvin was waiting by the car. What was he thinking? That he had found his way back to her? Was he filled with joy when he thought of this new meeting? During dinner at the Brandts', his tone had been friendly but discreet. He had told them about his roles in two small farces: *A Reluctant Tragic Hero* by Chekhov and *Playing with Fire* by Strindberg. He said the latter in Swedish and looked in Lydia's direction. Had she perhaps seen the play? No, she had not. The times when he had addressed her directly, it had always been with questions about her daily life, her work. And Lydia had answered with the same gentle distance. There was nothing awkward about their slight reserve in this second meeting, but Lydia did wonder if he was trying to keep her at a distance in order to spare her—in other words, out of consideration, as though the underlying message was that this could never be anything more than a friendly association. But then, to Lydia's relief, he asked if he could go with her the next time she went out to one of the farms. Not that that in itself was an invitation to something deeper or more intimate, but it did seem to open the space around them and certainly kept her expectations buoyant.

Lydia rinsed off her boots, then took the farmer by the hand. She was sorry about the dead calf. But he shook his head. She had saved the life of the other calf. A twin birth. And both had been lying in such awkward positions. Everything was at stake, but Lydia had not let it affect her. She had worked with determination, not desperation. As soon as the dead calf had been lifted away and placed on the dusty straw in a corner of the stall, she started to help the living calf into the world. And when all her efforts resulted in success, she stood bent double, out of breath, her hands on her knees. A trembling, unsteady creature and a pitiful carcass engulfed by flies were the day's sorry catch.

When the work was done, Edvin went home with Lydia. The surrounding countryside was bathed in a clear afternoon light. Lydia put a jug of cold water, two glasses, and a bottle of gin on the table. They drank without saying anything, without a word about how good it was to drink in the heat, the wholesome taste of juniper, and without mention of the good weather or how lush everything around them was. They lay down on the uncut grass, side by side, both with their hands behind their heads, both filled, it would seem, with an innocent reticence. Lydia wanted to move closer to him. She wanted to whisper something improper in his ear. In the car, Edvin had said he was glad he had gone with her. Not that he had any great knowledge of her profession, he said, but there was little doubt that she was exceptionally good at her job and the farmers held her in deep respect. The crowns of the trees rustled and whispered. There was something amenable about harvest days like this, they were so thin and transparent and slipped unnoticed over all that was worldly. It was as though the short summer was ruled by unfathomable principles. Lydia propped herself up on her elbows. She stole a look at him, this unknown man. He was lying with his eyes closed. If only he would take the opportunity to do something more than simply praise her abilities, she thought. Had he no intention of seducing her? Where did the coyness come from?

TORSTEN CASIMIR WILHELM FLORUSSON LILLIECRONA

The year passed, time carried with it a unique lightness that could not be smothered. Ordinary everyday life played on repeat—her work, the animals, the household tasks, and the changing weather—everything recapitulated, everything renewed itself. And then, eventually, spring returned. One Sunday morning, Lydia was woken by the magpies outside. She had soot on her eyelids. She switched on the bedside lamp and held it up. Her breath created small clouds that quickly evaporated. The flowery wallpaper shone with a peculiar damp paleness. Water was trickling and running down the walls. Cold drips in the bedroom. Barefoot, she crossed the floorboards and opened the front door, then carried on to the edge of the forest. The rowan tree was almost black, the sky white. Dagmar came to meet her, and Lydia asked where she was heading, but there was no answer. They wandered through the trees, hand in hand. Lydia had to stop on several occasions to remove the twigs that had stuck to the soles of her feet. A flurry of snowflakes settled on their faces. It was lovely, refreshing, deeply alive, no hostility. And her mother was alive in the same way that Lydia was alive. The two of them carried the same feeling—a deep peace. They emerged from the trees and stopped by a small stream, and Dagmar asked if Lydia knew what it meant, that they had found each other again. Now they would want for nothing. There was no shame in that. And even though they were equals in the dream, Lydia was not dead like her mother was dead, and she could not follow her into the dead places: the dead forest, the dead tree trunks, the dead winter light.

Lydia woke up for the second time that morning. She sat on the edge of the bed and listened quietly to Edvin's breathing, pearls of sweat had formed on his upper lip. She found a hair band in the drawer of her bedside table and tied up her hair, then tiptoed out to the kitchen. She stood for a while with the fridge door open but saw nothing that tempted her—a stick of celery, that was all, and breakfast was done. At home on the farm, her mother had pinned up an embroidered text above her father's place at the table, a verse neatly stitched in black, blue, and green thread. "My home is so humble, its door so low, but never a dearer dwelling I saw around all the green world," it said. Lydia had never asked where it came from, if it was inherited from her grandparents, or if her mother had bought it on one of her trips to Stockholm or at a local market. Nor did she know the origins of the text. It was not a Biblical quote, she was certain of that, one could tell from the formulation. For all she knew, it could be a passage from the popular Swedish canon, but she could not remember having come across it anywhere other than on the kitchen wall at home, and she was actually well-versed in old-fashioned lyrical stanzas.

She hummed the last line, "around all the green world," as she made the coffee. Edvin padded in. He put his arms around her. His stubble scratched her cheek. Then he stole a coffee bean and said something about seeing himself as a man of few words. Before Lydia could ask what he meant, he disappeared into the living room, the veranda door was opened, and moments later he appeared out on the grass. He was tall, had muscular arms and a robust neck that suggested strength. His hair was grey and messy in a way that made Lydia guess that he cut it himself. She was tempted to tap on the windowpane for no particular reason—it would be so wonderful to give expression, no matter how fleeting and insufficient, to her desire—but she refrained. He stood there with his back to her in a white short-sleeved vest and light blue pyjama bottoms. What was he thinking? It looked as though he was studying the trees, the branches. He was so polite, this Edvin, he always made sure to say something courteous and flattering, and behind these friendly comments lay the kind of tenderness a woman might feel if a man were to remove a thread that was stuck to her coat. But he certainly was not a man of few words, and not reserved by nature. He seemed so full of all kinds of things. Did Lydia know that the actor who played Uncle Melker in *Seacrow Island* was called Torsten Casimir Wilhelm Florusson Lilliecrona? Had she ever seen the film where two children make a secret and forbidden graveyard for small animals and insects? No, the main character, Dmitri Gurov, met the lady with the dog in Yalta, not Malta. And had Lydia read the book that ends in separation, dishonesty, and confusion?

No, she did not know that, she had forgotten that, and she had not seen, had not read. And yet, despite his enthusiasm, Lydia got the impression that Edvin was full of sorrow. Did he miss his wife? Was it a broken heart? Was he worried about her? Lydia got it into her head that she would ask him straight out. But when, and in what context, would a question like that fall naturally into the conversation? At the end of the day, they barely knew each other, and nothing was decided between them. It was true that they met as often as they could, they had the intimacy of old friends. But were they together now? Were they really together as a couple? Were they lovers? Lydia stepped back into the room when Edvin turned toward the house. She did not want him to see her, did not want him to be on guard because she was watching him. He seemed so conspicuous as he walked toward the house, as if the sunlight were pushing him, as if the sunlight were in him. She heard his footsteps on the veranda boards, brisk snaps. The wood should be oiled, it was high time. He came in, held her around the waist. He was going to take a shower, he said, but first he wanted to ask if they could go and visit her father. It would be such a wonderful trip. He had never been that far north in Sweden, and he loved long car journeys. Lydia asked if he was serious. He stroked her cheek and, without answering, disappeared into the bathroom. Lydia could not picture Edvin at the farm, could not imagine him in her childhood home, among all the dilapidated things. And her father, how would he react? She had never brought a boyfriend home. How did her parents feel about that? Why did they never ask? "My home is so humble, its door so low." Lydia stood still, several seconds passed without her moving at all. It was a form of disbelief, a naive skepticism directed at herself, as though she were thinking: No one must know who I am.

WHAT WAS IT
THAT GRIPPED HER?

Johan Erneman took a sip of coffee, then shook his head and repeated that it really had not been necessary for Lydia and Edvin to drive all that way with no other purpose than to say hello. Was it because Lydia thought he was unable to manage alone? He did not need help with anything. They had sat down around the table on the terrace where Lydia and her parents used to sit an eternity ago, or so it felt. Lydia had made rhubarb soup, and they all helped themselves generously. She was sitting so close to her father that she could smell his fresh breath. He had always taken good care of his teeth, she thought. That was where she got it from. Edvin kept saying how wonderful he thought the farm was, and Johan was obviously very pleased. He pointed and explained, told them about a number of plans. He was doing the best he could, he said. Busy from morning to evening. There was no one else to do things for him. Lydia could see that her father was in good spirits, and soon enough a bottle of aquavit appeared on the table. They clinked glasses, cheered, and drank, drank until the bottle was empty. Not once did her father ask what Edvin did or where he came from. The farm and farming were the entirety of the conversation, and the mountains, the weather, the infernal power plant, the tractor. He used Edvin's surname on the few occasions he addressed his guest directly. Was Malm tired after the long journey? If Malm would like another shot? And Edvin adapted to his manner without any effort: Erneman had done a good job with the new windows. Erneman had been right to keep the old tractor. John Deere knew their stuff, and 130 horsepower was more than enough. He is just humouring him, Lydia thought, and so what—the atmosphere was easy and her father looked like he was enjoying himself.

It was only dark for an hour or two, as if the summer night closed its eyes and dropped off for a moment. Lydia went to get a woollen blanket from the chest in the living room and wrapped it around herself. She pulled her knees up under her chin and sat there listening. A moth flapped in her face. She waved it away with her hand. The two men stood talking with their backs to her. Their hair was illuminated by the outside light, and bluish cigarette smoke swirled around them. Her father spoke with a familiarity, like an officer who had just praised a soldier for his endurance or courage. Lydia could not make out what he was saying, only the odd phrase here and there: "It was a tragic case," "the poor thing had a stomach tumour." Then Edvin pointed to the mountain ridge, and Johan nodded and said something about a pair of binoculars. He disappeared into the house, and when he came back, Lydia took the opportunity to retire. She wanted to get some sleep. Edvin gave her a hug, her father said a brusque goodnight and then looked through the binoculars.

The upstairs bedroom was warm and stuffy. Lydia opened the window and fastened the latch. She could hear her father's voice below: but one does not speak of the rope in a hanged man's house. She had never experienced him like this before. All his stiffness and restraint had vanished. He stood there chatting away to Edvin, a stranger, and was friendliness itself. Lydia lay down under the duvet and, out of old habit, folded her hands, but without praying for anything. She soon fell asleep to the murmuring voices outside, and it was as though someone sat down on the edge of her bed and whispered: I've got a story to tell.

A horse came trotting down the country road. A grey and dirty work horse. It kicked up the dust. Its movements were elaborate and angular and as if it were made from granite. Was it pulling a cart? Yes, of course it was pulling a cart. A cart? Or a wagon? A simple wooden bed with wheels underneath, and a girl was sitting at the back dangling her legs over the edge, and the girl was on her way to swim in a pool. The forest pool was warm and full of weeds. Her mother had said it was healthy and good for the constitution, and her mother had grown up and lived in these parts all her life, so she should know. The girl jumped down from the vehicle and ran light-footed and unafraid over a bridge of dilapidated, rotten planks; the muddy water gurgled in gasps and sighs. And soon she lay down on the forest floor. The slender pine trees above her sprinkled pollen through the light, in the same way the horse had kicked up the dust on the track, and it was as though she entreated the silence or infatuation or growing desire that she still only spoke of quietly to herself, this desire that called her, that said "now," that said "come," that said "no, not yet." What was it that gripped her so? Simply to be full of this, the comfort that lives so powerfully inside: to exist in the summer light.

IN AN ENCHANTED FOREST SHE PAUSED FOR THOUGHT

A s often as it was possible, Edvin took the train from town in order to spend time with Lydia. There was no fuss involved, or so it seemed, and Lydia looked forward to his presence. The days before they were to meet could not pass quickly enough. One of the things that impressed Lydia was how handy and able he was. He liked to work in the garden behind the house. He looked after the various bushes and beds and vines with care, and all the herbs and flowers that were there flourished and grew in colourful clusters. He had no difficulty in getting up early; even on days off when there were no obligations, he woke at around five and lay in bed reading until Lydia stirred, or he got up and went for a walk, came back energized, made breakfast. But Lydia was who she was. She constantly found herself fretting and pondering. How could something like this last? Even in the most unassuming situations, she was conscious of the pitiful possibilities that lay in a relationship between two people. Lydia abhorred these qualms of hers, wished to free herself from them, but had no idea how. Edvin had in a way already disappeared from her life once before, and even now when all the reasons and causes had been sorted, there was an inherent deficit in their relationship. On the other hand: was it really worth the trouble to dwell on it? It was as though she were challenging the reality that would not comply with her own wishes, as both her will and wishes pulled toward Edvin. The days when he was not with her, she worked. She was active and enterprising, took all the shifts she could. This was perhaps to burn off some of the doubts she harboured. Whatever the case, Edvin's affection seemed steady. He had an easy and amenable nature, and that suited Lydia. With him she had both the bond and the independence she wanted. And the fact that a week or two might pass without them meeting did not matter; to the contrary, that was perhaps precisely why they found peace in each other's company. They walked along the roads or went for long hikes in the forest. There was something unambiguous and easy between them. They talked openly about whatever was on their minds, all manner of things. They went shopping and made food together. Edvin always listened to audio plays while they prepared their meals, and Lydia found the old recordings enjoyable. It was not until the late summer that Edvin suggested they should perhaps move in together— properly, as he said. They were sitting eating dinner. It was raining outside. He would love to live in the country. And commuting to and from town and the theatre was not a problem. But for reasons that were unclear to her, Lydia could not imagine the two of them living in the same house. So that he wouldn't feel more embarrassed than necessary, she pretended at first not to have heard what he said. She asked if he would like the rest of the wine and poured it into his glass before he could answer. There were times when she wished she was more uninhibited, and this was certainly one. She then asked later if they could perhaps give it more time, she was unable to think of anything better, and he replied that of course they could give it more time. More time? Lydia was annoyed. Her request was as empty as it was inadequate, and she was afraid it would detract from what they had together. Her skepticism was like a loose door that constantly blew open. It had to yield, it had to let go of her, she had to let go of it. Why could she not simply accept him? What was getting in the way? Lydia found herself thinking that she was like one of those obstinate farmers. She remembered one in particular who had angered her. He had a farm where children from the city could experience a ride in a horse and cart, or a sleigh. And then, of all things, he had harnessed up a pregnant mare to a heavy load. And it all became too much for the poor animal, out in the forest, and she lay down to foal in among all the sleighs and torches and hysterical children. Fortunately, both the mare and the foal survived, but Lydia could not free herself from the thought that she too suffered from the same confounded stubbornness. She grabbed her wineglass, which was empty, and drank the dregs, unexpectedly knocking the stem against the side of her plate as she put it back down. She said something peculiar, it just popped out: It's not exactly as if one were walking in an enchanted forest. And Edvin looked at her, puzzled. What on earth did she mean? She wanted to keep the house, she said. He would have to move in with her. Did he want to? Yes, he wanted to. He wanted to live with her and learn to know her more, and she need not worry, she could keep all her idiosyncrasies. Lydia felt that these slightly too smooth words were said in a strange order, but let it lie. Ever since she was a child, she had suspected that everyone she met would be like one another, unless she found ways to renew them, and the secret, she had discovered, was quite simply to renew herself—well, simply, there was nothing simple about changing oneself; nothing is obvious if one wants to transform oneself.

A QUESTION

The autumn came early, in the beginning of September, almost overnight the air cooled, the days shortened, and soon the leaves blushed on the trees up the gentle hill-sides. On a morning filled with steady rain, Lydia came to a small, poorly maintained farm, a place she had never been before. The road that wound its way into the pine forest was narrow and muddy as a cattle track, and Lydia had to walk the final stretch up to the ridge where the farm lay. The house was brownish red, like coagulated blood, she thought, and piti-ful. An old lady stood in the doorway, small and stooped. No animals, no children, no husband: just the one dog that was sleeping so heavily. The woman said she could not wake it.

In the hall, some old skis and poles leaned against the wall. The dust spun lazily in the half-light. There was a smell of coffee, a burnt and sweet smell. Embroidered pictures with quotes from the Bible and hunting scenes hung side by side on the wall, and rows of stuffed birds and small animals stood displayed on two mahogany shelves. In Lydia's mind, people, events, even abstract concepts, often appeared as images. And this house, this woman's home, was not only an illustration of obvious decay, it was also a portrait of a lonely life. But what did it encompass, this loneliness? What did it consist of? Presumably it also had components, limbs and organs. The old woman had wandered into it, at a ruthlessly slow pace; at some point, a given moment, perhaps already in childhood, the knowledge that there was no retreat had become indisputable. Lydia pictured an uneven, greasy pencil line, like a carpenter's marker on a plank.

In a basket under the kitchen table lay a dog, a golden Labrador. Lydia saw straightaway that life had abandoned it. The body collapsed, the twisted limbs stiff. It was a sad discovery. She knew all too well what a dog could mean for an old person. What should she say? Simply that it was dead? She crouched down and stroked the animal, as though, in that way, to delay or at least soften the blow that had to come. The woman asked if there was anything the vet could do. The dog often whimpered in its sleep, as though dreaming, but now had slept heavily without moving for more than twenty-four hours. Lydia stood up, took a few steps back, not so much to gain an overview as to win more time. The woman looked at her with suspicion. No, she wanted to know now, but clearly did not want to know all the same, because just as Lydia was about to tell her, the old woman disappeared out of the kitchen, sobbing. Lydia waited for a short while before she followed her and sat down beside her outside on the step. The woman grasped Lydia's hand, as a sign of trust, and told her that her sight was poor. She generally screwed up her eyes and used sound and smell to get her bearings. She thought illness and death smelled horrible. Illness smelled of decay and damp rust. A stable smelled good, but a cowshed was different, confusion reigned in a cowshed: chemicals, muck, and soured milk. Lydia squeezed the woman's hand gently. The vet smelled good, said the woman. What was the vet's name? Lydia. Ah, Lydia, that was a good name. She herself was called Anna. She stood up. Men reeked of tobacco, she said. Then she stumbled back into the house.

They buried the dog together. Lydia dug a hole at the bottom of the grassy slope, they wrapped the retriever in a worn wax cloth, and laid it in the thick earth. There was no need for a cross; however, Lydia was welcome to say a few words, as she knew so much about animals. But Lydia was not able to gather her thoughts. She could not think of a suitable verse. She stood there and waited, there was a certain courage in being able to wait. She eventually placed her arm around the old woman's shoulders, and suddenly she remembered a short line or two that would have to do:

> Are you so poor, wee darling,
> Are you as sad as they say?

Anna said something about the human voice being like handwriting, and Lydia's handwriting was a little too controlled, she said, a little too restrained, but that was also good as that meant it was clear and easy to read. This made Lydia laugh. She was both embarrassed and pleased. There was something appealing about the woman. She was direct in a way that meant one did not lose face. One was seen but not watched, and Lydia felt there was an important distinction in that. Her sympathy only increased when Anna pre-empted her by saying she needn't worry. The old woman was not going to tidy and wash the house. She was not going to sit down and mope and miss the dog. But if Lydia came across another one that needed a home, could she please say? Anna had to have a dog. After all, she had always had a dog. Ever since she was a young girl, with long black hair, who ran everywhere, she had always had a four-legged companion. One need never doubt what to do then. She had been a wild child, she said, more passionate than refined.

Only when Lydia got back into the car did she realize how wet and cold she was. She looked in the mirror. Her hair was tangled with rain, her face pale. She decided to go home and take a warm bath before going back to the clinic. She felt a defiant delight, an almost inadmissible joy took hold of her. And when she was home again and sank down into the bath, she closed her eyes and pictured the woman in the brownish-red house. Anna was standing motionless by the kitchen window, looking down toward the grassy slope where the dog lay as motionless in the ground. It would be an exaggeration, but by no means wrong, to say that a dignity was now apparent in her face. But what was she thinking? What struck her as true or false, possible or impossible? And Edvin? What was Edvin doing? What was he doing right now? Was he thinking of her with desire? And what about her father? Was he gathering the last aronia berries from the red hedge down by the road? And what was Dagmar up to? Was she walking through the forest? Did she emerge into a clearing? Did she stop to listen? Did she hear an eagle owl hoot?

.

DREAM-HOLD-DOOR

One night, Lydia had a curious dream. She was wandering around in a forest, an unknown forest that was cut through by streams and turbulent rivers. Without knowing how, she had got lost in unexplored territory, and it was full of dead trees and thick, decaying undergrowth, rotten tree trunks everywhere. She tried as best she could to pick her way through the tangle, had to clamber over stumps and trunks, break off twigs and push prickly, reluctant branches to one side. Finally she was clear of the tough terrain and found herself by a river, and an empty raft floated slowly by. It floated in a straight line, as though it were following some kind of mechanical track under the water. Lydia got it into her head that she wanted to board the vessel. She started to wade out into the water, swam and struggled, and finally managed to make her way out to the abandoned raft; then, as is normally the way, she heaved herself up without any fuss and lay down on her back to enjoy the sight of the tree crowns and blue sky. But soon the sunlight was so blinding that she had to cover her eyes with her hands. She lifted herself up on her knees. The raft started to pitch heavily. A rapid sucked it along, tossing and turning it midstream. At first Lydia thought she would sink, that she was in danger of going under, but after a couple of collisions with stones and a breathless dip, it bounced up again. And now it was as though the raft were growing up from the water. It bobbed like a bird on the white crests of the waves, then eventually sailed into smaller waterways and got stuck in the shallows between two boulders. Dandelion seeds swirled in the air, the dappled sunlight spilled through the crowns of the trees that had grown together high overhead, like the roof of a cathedral.

Lydia was in no way superstitious, only sometimes a dream could be so lifelike, and one afternoon when she was painting the kitchen, her mother rang, and even though it was inconvenient, Lydia answered the call. She tucked the telephone in between her shoulder and her cheek and asked what her mother was up to, as the line was a bit fuzzy. Her mother said she was painting the kitchen, and Lydia replied she was doing the very same thing. She was about to put the last coat on the window frames. Ah, the window frames, her mother said, they were always so tricky, she no longer had a steady hand. Were they really each standing by the kitchen window painting on white gloss? Johan was on his way, her mother could tell her. He had been to the shop. And no sooner had she said that than a message pinged on Lydia's phone. It was Edvin. He would be leaving town in ten minutes, was there anything he should buy?

SHE WOKE UP HAPPY, WITHOUT KNOWING WHY

On the mornings that Edvin was with her, Lydia woke close to him, it was not so much a matter of drowsy caresses, she clung to him, held his body so tight her muscles ached. She felt an apology was needed; after all, it must have disturbed his sleep. But he dismissed it as nothing. Of course he had slept, he assured her. He was always so well rested after his nights with her. It was not always he found the same peace in his apartment in town. He could lie there, tossing and turning far into the night, kept awake by the incessant noise, the steady hum that never died. He had recently taken on new work at the theatre. In addition to his allocated roles, he was given the go-ahead when he asked if he could direct Strindberg's *The First Warning*, and even though it was a short one-act play, it required that he work late into the evenings.

Lydia was delighted that Edvin was so practical. She had already noticed this the first winter they were together. He would sneak out of bed as early as five in the morning, and soon after she heard the crackle and roar of the wood stove in the living room through the door that had been left ajar. There was a strange ambiguity about him. She thought that her father, who undeniably was also assiduous and good with his hands, so easily made her feel impotent. Already as a child she had been ashamed of him. He could come into the kitchen where she and her mother were having supper, his shirt smeared and filthy with engine oil or elk blood, and the pungent smell made her lose her appetite. There was no point in saying anything either, as he would then just launch into a spiel about all that he had to think about, that he had not done this or that for his own sake, and could they not perhaps show him a smidgen of gratitude. Her father's strength and versatility were mechanical and unpractical. He busied himself with so many laborious tasks. Piles of planks and boxes and tools to move here and there, the house was constantly being renovated, walls built and torn down, and most of the work was left half-done. Lydia could hardly bear to think how many hours had been spent on measuring, mending, and carpentry. In contrast to her father, Edvin was quick to see what was needed, what could be improved or repaired. There was never any discussion, never any fuss. He did the work with an apprentice's charming desire to show off his skill. And Lydia appreciated all the bits and pieces he did around the house, everything he sorted: a hole in the eavestrough, a leaking washer, a loose door handle; nothing was left undone or to fall into disrepair. And he did this work quietly, as though it was purely reflex, something he drew strength from. Lydia thought she was perhaps unfair to her father, who undoubtedly had meant well. As he saw it, he had only been doing his duty. His job was to provide for his wife and daughter and ensure that the farm did not decline, all of this to win their respect. But as the obstinate, unpractical man that he was, his efforts seemed more like a game, like a string of obvious and entrenched bad habits.

SHE WAS NOT
GOING TO
THINK ABOUT IT

Even before the doctor confirmed it, Lydia knew she was carrying a child. She could feel it; sleep was more evasive, the working day harder, she had to concentrate where previously it was a matter of routine: cleaning a wound, checking a litter of puppies, putting down an ailing rabbit. Late one evening, only a few days after she had been to the doctor and had the pregnancy confirmed, she found herself at one of the farms. She stood in the pigsty and stared at the boar and could not remember why she had been called there. To compose herself, she rattled off a couple of givens: the nights were starting to get cold, and the pig would continue to put on weight until Christmas. And then she remembered: it was to be vaccinated and weighed. She decided it was time to tell Edvin about the child. Why she had not shared this with him straightaway was unclear. Perhaps because she felt it had to implant itself. After all, it was still very early in the pregnancy. It was not something she had kept secret from him for weeks. This short time for reflection could be justified. Edvin was in town to collect the last of his belongings. She would tell him as soon as he came back. She still had not visited him there.

The flat was in the east of Oslo, she knew that but was not very familiar with the city, had only been there briefly a couple of times. And she still had not been to the theatre to see him in one of the roles that earned him such praise in the newspapers.

Edvin's reaction was both strange and intuitive. He dropped the last moving box to the floor with a small thud, put his arms around her, said nothing at first, just stood there and hugged her tight. After a minute or so he relaxed and became heavier, as though he wanted to rest following great physical exertion. Lydia pressed her face into his chest, butting him gently once or twice, then asked what he thought. He said she must not for a moment believe that he was wavering. The fact that she was pregnant was a blessing. His breath was ragged, released in small bursts, and Lydia could not rid herself of the thought that he was a little frightened by the whole thing. But she did not want to ask him. With a caress, she freed herself from his embrace and asked if they should find the best place for his things so the boxes would not need to be left standing around. And while they were at it, they could go to buy more bookshelves. No, no, he would rather get the materials from the timberyard so he could build the shelves himself, made to measure from floor to ceiling and solid. Lydia asked him to take the measurements he needed. She would be more than happy to help him build shelves along one of the walls in the living room, where they would easily have room for about a thousand novels, one only had to cast an eye over all the boxes marked *Books* to realize that they would definitely need all those shelves. Edvin pulled the tape off one of the boxes and took out a random book. He held it up for Lydia to see and said it was a fantastic novel, then he leafed through it and read: "But what she wants is nothing more or less than a miracle." And Lydia nodded and told him she had read it when she was young, as it was written by a well-loved author. Edvin went into the kitchen. He cut an orange into boats and shared them with her. Lydia looked at him with affection but not complete sincerity. Could the sum of all the right choices still be defeat? They stood and sucked in the fruit juice, and then, without warning, it was as though an unintended cheerfulness filled the distance between them. Lydia dribbled, dried her chin on her sleeve. She asked him to tell her something, tell her anything, about himself, about his work, about the films he liked, the books. No matter if she had heard it before. Nothing dramatic or sad had happened, nothing had befallen them, and yet it was as though she had uttered a desire to return to simpler times. Edvin bit into the orange peel. He understood perhaps what she was thinking, because he said she needn't worry. She should not fret so much. If she got fed up with him, he promised to leave. But one does not choose, he said, one is given a gift, and whatever one forgets or neglects, one is spared. Lydia was not sure that she quite understood what he meant, and yet: if she had understood correctly, she was not convinced that he was right.

SHORT
INTERMISSION

I t was a cold and clear afternoon. The air hung frosty-blue over the gulleys and slopes and great, towering snowdrifts; the berms left by snowplows were so high on many of the small roads that it was dangerous to drive along them. The snow had come early and in vast quantities, and by the time the Christmas month approached, it lay so heavy that the trees were bent, the hedges mercilessly crushed, and the bushes had long since vanished beneath windswept frozen wastes. The farmers struggled to keep access to the farms clear and had to regularly brush snow from the roofs. There were periods when the tractors and snowplows were out day and night. Lydia and Edvin had also been up on the roof and cleared a colossal, frozen drift that hung precariously over the eavestrough. And as if all the snow was not enough trouble, sudden gusts of strong wind swept across the open landscape.

One morning Lydia was called to examine an elk that had been run over. As soon as she pulled the hood of her parka over her head and opened the front door, the wind charged in, blowing open the door to the hallway and the kitchen, and before she could close the front door behind her, she heard one of the upstairs doors slam.

The accident had happened on one of the many forest roads. An unflagging farmer had been out early in the morning to clear the roads and the elk was in a terrible state, having been hit by the tractor: its hind legs were crushed, its back presumably broken, and the sharp plow had made a long and deep cut in its belly as though the animal were to be flayed. The unfortunate man stood there with an open shotgun over his shoulder. A grisly crime scene, Lydia thought as she crouched down in the bloody snow. She could tell straight-away that the blood pumping out of the wound was from the lungs, an unmistakable dark colour. She asked the farmer to do the deed, and he did not hesitate. He snapped the shotgun together, positioned himself, and aimed both barrels at the animal's head. The mutilated body continued to move. One of the back legs kicked uncontrollably. A reflex in death that Lydia never quite got used to.

AN OX
AND AN ASS

The day before Christmas Eve, early in the morning, Lydia drove over to see Anna, the woman in the forest. It was a detour, as she really had nothing to do there, but in the spirit of the time of year, she wanted to see the old lady. Fortunately the snow had been cleared all the way up to the house, and she only had to walk the short distance from the gate to the door. When she knocked, there was no answer. She tried the door handle. The door was locked. Then she noticed a trail of shuffling footsteps in the snow and followed it around to the back of the house and on into the frozen spruce trees. What was the old woman up to? For a moment, Lydia was worried. But then she pushed a low-hanging branch to one side and spotted a figure bending over out in a clearing where the trees had been felled. Lydia called and Anna straightened up. Goodness, had the vet come to visit her? What a lovely surprise. What did the vet want? Lydia explained that she had been doing something in the vicinity and decided to pop in. Anna had cut down a tree but misjudged the height. Now it was lying there deep in the snow and she was unable to move it. Lydia took hold of the lower part of the trunk and weighed it in her hands. Anna handed her the axe, and the length was halved.

Back at the house, Lydia put up the tree in the stand that Anna had already positioned behind the sofa, and now that it was inside in the warmth, the needles soon started to give off a cozy scent, as reassuring as the smell of hay in a stable. Anna made a pot of coffee and put out a plate of biscuits. She said that she had a sleigh. It was in the outhouse. She wanted Lydia to have it. Then Lydia could take her husband and children on a torch-lit sleigh ride between Christmas and New Year. Did Lydia have a husband and children? Lydia was not sure what to say. Yes, there was a man, it was true, and a child on the way. She put a hand on her stomach, which was not yet big enough to reveal her secret. But she was certainly not going to accept the sleigh. If Anna no longer had any use for it, Lydia would buy it. But Anna insisted, she really did not have any use for it now and it also badly needed an overhaul. No, Lydia must accept it as a gift, otherwise it would go to a rummage sale.

After coffee and a couple of biscuits, Lydia helped to decorate the tree. Anna was adamant there was no need to let it dry out anymore. Lydia opened the two cardboard boxes that sat on the dining table. The antique glass baubles felt brittle and delicate in her hands. They must have reflected so many celebrations. Lydia hung them up with the greatest care. She found herself studying the old woman through the branches and needles. Anna seemed content, focused as she was on this seasonal activity. Lydia was struck by how protective the rural isolation actually was; even the loss of her dog did not appear to have disrupted Anna's existence. Once the star had been placed on top of the tree, Anna put in the plug to test it, and every single one of the small bulbs lit up and filled the semi-darkness with a warm glow. And when Lydia was ready to go and went to put on her coat, Anna pointed to the crib she had assembled on the bureau. Like an earnest schoolgirl, she explained that neither the ox nor the ass was mentioned in the Gospel of Luke, but Isaiah mentioned them both: "The ox knoweth his owner, and the ass his master's crib: but Israel doth not know, my people doth not consider," she quoted. In addition to Joseph and Mary and the babe, the crib included several other figurines: shepherds and sheep, camels and servants, angels and wise men; they were all carved from wood, and well worn at that, cracked with flaking paint, even the star of Bethlehem lacking its usual lustre. Lydia pushed her feet down into her boots and took her parka off the peg. She did not get much further. Anna backed into the living room in a rather bizarre fashion and plumped down on the nearest chair. She felt rather odd, she said. Lydia dropped down in front of her and found her pulse. A slight trembling, that was all. The old woman's face was cold and waxen. Remember the sleigh, she rattled. It was a gift. If the vet made sure to catch the 19:23 train from Lausanne, she would be in Geneva by midnight. And it would be easy to find accommodation and a cheap, warming meal. Lydia put a finger to her lips. For the first time, her job was not to save the life of an animal, but of a person.

A HASTY
YOUNG WOMAN

Lydia sat on an uncomfortable plastic chair and waited to hear what the doctors had to say about Anna's condition. Anna's family name was Schou, and she had spent her early adult life in Switzerland, Brandt had told Lydia. Anna came to the area in her fifties and was now over eighty. In Switzerland, yes. Anna had lived up in the mountains in a collective together with a young man she had met on a train journey through Italy. It was an insular life, but it seemed to have suited her perfectly. What was it she wanted to escape? The family's expectations? She had grown up in a wealthy home in Bærum, just outside Oslo. But apparently she had been a wild and impetuous child, and as a teenager, one escapade followed another.

A Christmas tree twinkled in the children's ward, and the walls were adorned with shiny paper chains and drawings of Santa Claus and angels. Why were they always blond, these bewinged beings? Lydia thought she should ring Edvin. She had turned off her mobile phone, and he probably wondered what had happened to her. On the other hand: he was used to waiting for her, and they were not in the habit of calling when there was no need. I am here, and I am staying here, she thought. Finally a doctor came and told her that Anna had had a stroke, but there was no cause for concern as the effects of the ruptured blood vessel were mild.

By the time Lydia got home, it was well past midnight. Edvin was asleep on the sofa. She stroked his upper arm. The strain of the day had drained her of energy. She crept into his warm body, and he put his arms around her with a drowsy contentedness, held her tight as though she might bolt, but she did not want to bolt, she wanted to be kissed, not too passionately, but for a long time, even if only a stationary kiss, an equitable, easy, even indifferent caress, nothing to discover, like a schoolchild's simple secrets. Afterwards she told him, in mumbling broad strokes, why she had been delayed, and because she was relieved, she could say that it was as though Anna had been getting ready to say her farewells, but now had sat down again. Edvin went to find a blanket, which he placed over Lydia. With great care he put a cushion under her head and then he sat down on the chair by the fireplace. The embers were about to die out, and there was only a faint glow. Every so often a red flame flared up, like an unrestrained exhale. Would she like something to eat? He made her some tea and bread and cheese, but when he came back and put the plate down in front of her, she was asleep.

On Christmas Eve, Lydia woke later than usual. Her sleep had been full of dreams, almost conscious, as though illuminated from within. She got up, stretched her body, touched her belly impatiently. Entering the Christmas spirit and being with child—the one was associated with the other, she thought, in the same way that one recognizes youthful fantasies of an embrace when one experiences one's first real kiss. The crackling of the fire, the smell of freshly ground coffee. And was there not something else too? A sweet, spicy scent. Like a curious child, she went to the kitchen to investigate, and there they were, plump pepper cakes, their softness intact. Edvin opened the oven door, pulled out one tray, and put in another. He dried his hands and gave her a hug. Through the kitchen window, Lydia could see the snow being driven by the wind and how it drifted up the west-facing wall of the house. She went to the bathroom for her morning wash. She whistled on her way up the stairs. She got it into her head that they could go to church. They would get there on time if she got a move on. Lydia was not religious, that time was well past, and anyway, that kind of faith had never really taken root in her. But some of the stories in the Bible still moved her, not in a sentimental way, but rather as intelligent and perceptive principles. One should strive to find "the Good" in oneself and in others, as best one could. The most important thing, what characterized her, was her sense that everything around her, all the life, everything that fought to stay alive, must have been created. She hoped that that was the case, almost believed— that there was a creator behind it all, that something one might call a forgiving love existed, that miracles were possible, salvation. She did, on occasion, pray, always with caution and, of all things, a degree of skepticism, but she did sometimes fold her hands and express a wish, a hope, or thanks. Ach, she did not want to go to church now, after all. She would phone her father. She wanted to get it over and done with. It had been a while since they had spoken together. She had not even told him she was expecting a child. It took a while for Johan to answer. She wished him a happy Christmas, but he was sullen and wary, as though he had a daughter who was always begging for money or never stopped asking about her inheritance. She asked how he was. There was no real answer, just a few absurd remarks about a local boundary dispute. Lydia felt ashamed. She was ashamed for having expected more, if only a well-intended comment, something easy to understand and personal, certainly something more than these empty words that he knew had nothing to do with her. She rested her elbows on the sink, leaned forward in a position both strained and uncomfortable. And then she chose defiance. She told him she was pregnant. Yes, she was expecting a baby, and even though she did not know if it was a boy or a girl they were expecting, it just fell out of her mouth that it was a girl, a daughter, and no sooner had she said it than she envisaged the girl. Look, there she was, picking gooseberries from the small bushes behind the house. There she was, sitting on the front step picking at a scab. There she was, running through the sun-filled rooms. And Lydia thought that nothing could eclipse such confidence. But what would she be called? Would she be called Dagmar? No, that would have to wait.

PLAY

Lydia quickly found her seat in the small theatre auditorium, but it was only when darkness fell on the audience and the lights on the stage went up that she noticed the heavy, almost vulgar perfume, not dissimilar to dying black dogwood blossom. At first it was simply horrible, but then she got used to it. It helped to think that perhaps it was the pregnancy that had made her more sensitive. She had felt so peculiar out there in the foyer as well, not uncomfortable, far from it, it was more physical, a tiredness and unfamiliar heaviness in her limbs. But now she was looking forward to seeing Edvin onstage. She had only been in a theatre a couple of times before. The first was in Stockholm. She had been in her early teens when she went with her mother to spend a few days of the holiday in the capital and to see a production of Selma Lagerlöf's *Dunungen*. And many years later, while she was still working for Stangel, she had gone to see *The Swedenhielms* in Malmö, together with a friend from her student days at the University of Agricultural Sciences in Ultuna.

Edvin was not someone who talked about his roles. When he was in rehearsal, he would walk around with a script, mumbling. Lydia would often hear him upstairs in the study, and if the weather was good, he lay out in the hammock. Once, while she was weeding the herb bed, she overheard a telephone conversation through the open kitchen window. Edvin was talking about Ibsen. He would love to see a production where Hedda Tesman's fatal choice was not included. He thought that the "shooting episode," as he called it, was an artificial premise. And as for *Little Eyolf*, he said very condescendingly that it was Ibsen's *Beyond Our Power*, yes, it was Ibsen's Bjørnson play. It was the only time Lydia had experienced Edvin as crass and sarcastic.

It felt very odd to see him appear on the stage. Like a pantomime artist, he stepped onto the stage through an invisible door. He seemed to just appear from the darkness and suddenly stood there fully illuminated. He looked incredibly handsome, Lydia thought. A woman made a similar entrance through another invisible passage. She yawned and sang softly to herself—was it German she was singing? And she was beautiful, beautiful and dressed all in white, cool in the artificial dawn light. Edvin, also dressed in white, in what looked like a linen suit, said good morning and asked if she had slept well, and she replied that she had slept splendidly given the circumstances. "Given the circumstances": the conflict was mentioned already in the second line, like some heralded and evident declaration. Lydia had always found plays a little comical—comical or touching. No matter how masterful and realistic the play was, it still consisted of lines spoken in a contrived drama, there was always an overarching intention behind it all, a score, a given framework for the marionettes. What unfolded on a stage and was shown to the world came from a more pure and false state than reality; the movements and dialogues were based on assumptions other than those in daily life. But what did that matter? Because despite the artificiality, despite the almost charming rituals onstage, even the most detailed portrayals were ultimately about understanding earthly conditions, the human condition. Lydia thought about her mother and the evenings they spent together listening to the radio. Had it not been Gunnar Björnstrand and Eva Dahlbeck who played the husband and wife in the radio play? And was it not Ingmar Bergman who had directed it? Lydia put her right hand under her round belly, weighed it carefully, felt a kick. Was Edvin thinking about the child there onstage? Was the thought of impending fatherhood a source of joy for him?

FROM AUGUST STRINDBERG'S *THE FIRST WARNING* — A COMEDY IN ONE ACT

WIFE: Yes! It has been well proved that your love loses its fervour the moment you have no reason to be jealous. Do you remember last summer, when there was not a soul on that island but we two? You were away all day, fishing, hunting, getting up an appetite, putting on flesh—and developing a self-assurance that was almost insulting. HUSBAND: And yet I recall being jealous—of the hired man. WIFE: Merciful heavens! HUSBAND: Yes, I noticed that you couldn't give him an order without making conversation; that you couldn't send him out to cut some wood without first having inquired about the state of his health, his future prospects, and his love affairs…You are blushing, I think? WIFE: Because I am ashamed of you…HUSBAND:…Who…WIFE: …Has no sense of shame whatever. HUSBAND: Yes, so you say. But will you please tell me why you hate me? WIFE: I don't hate you. I simply despise you! Why? Probably for the same reason I despise all men as soon as they—what do you call it?—are in love with me. I am like that, and I can't tell why. HUSBAND: So I have observed, and my warmest wish has been that I might hate you, so that you might love me. Woe is the man who loves his own wife! WIFE: Yes, you are to be pitied, and so am I, but what can be done? HUSBAND: Nothing. We have roved and roamed for seven years, hoping that some circumstance, some chance, might bring about a change. I have tried to fall in love with others and have failed. In the meantime, your eternal contempt and my own continued ridiculousness have stripped me of all courage, all faith in myself, all power to act. Six times I have run away from you—and now I shall make my seventh attempt. *He rises and picks up the travelling bag.* WIFE: So those little trips of yours were attempts to run away? HUSBAND: Futile attempts! The last time I got as far as Genoa. I went to the galleries but saw no pictures—only you. I went to the opera but heard nobody—only your voice behind every note. I went to a Pompeian café, and the one woman who pleased me looked like you—or seemed to do so later.[1]

1 Translated by Edwin Björkman, 1916, https://www.gutenberg.org/files/44302/44302-h/44302-h.htm#THE_FIRST_WARNING

FOREST INTERIOR WITH SWALLOWS AFTER RAIN

Lydia had stopped the car on a soft, muddy forest track, and then she heard a sound. It was both insistent and feeble at the same time, as though a gust of wind or a bird were searching blindly through the treetops. Searching for what? For spring? Some comfort in the damp, shivering air? And no matter how ridiculous the thought was, she felt it was imperative that she find out where the unidentified sound was coming from. She trudged along the side ditch and off into the trees, birch suckers everywhere and sticky bracken left from the year before. Was it an insect? It was now more like several layered sounds, cheerful and shy, as though they were playing around, mischievous and teasing. An excavator started up on one of the farms, and even though it was far way, it erased the sound of the bird, because it had to be a bird. Lydia went deeper into the forest, pushed her way through a hazel thicket, kept one hand on her belly, and scrambled up a steep slope. She came to a lookout point, a small clearing where moss covered the rotting stumps of felled trees. When she was a child in Jämtland, the endless forest had felt claustrophobic to her, those dark, northern forests that ran from the Caucasus to the North Sea; now she looked out over the waving deciduous trees, and even though they had neither buds nor green leaves, their rounded crowns swayed gently: oak trees, chestnut trees, elm and ash and birch; transparent, full of anticipation. Lydia sometimes thought that it was not time that changed her so much as space: the forest floor, the ridge of the hill, the garden and herb bed, the kitchen table full of chanterelle mushrooms spread out to dry, the wallpaper in the nursery, the living room where her mother had just fallen asleep, the banks of a dry, summer river, the riverbed, the loft where she was sure she had seen an owl, the student apartment where she had made love for the first time. Time is blind, without consideration, space has eyes that are always open, a memory that keeps reality alive.

There is a gravity that comes from the earth
As it hides so many dead.
It's so beautiful, the meadow, its beauty so bright.
It's the gravity of the roots that makes the crown bright.

Lydia spent a lot of time at the clinic, and the tasks were generally trivial, nothing more than routine: cats with stomach upsets, overweight dogs, the occasional unwell guinea pig. Then, when the hectic lambing season started, she insisted on joining in, and criss-crossed the district with Brandt in order to welcome the bewildered creatures. And then summer came, the warm days of July, and with the summer came an impatience, guessing and apprehension. She imagined it was a girl she was carrying, and in the peculiar and persistent visions that filled her night and day, the girl was seven or eight years old, and the most curious thing of all: she roamed around inside Lydia, under the taut dome of her stomach. She was in a forest, or by a river, or on top of a hill. Sitting, sleeping, or walking around. It was as though Lydia could hear her shouts from inside: playful and in passing, like swallows around the gables of an evening. And she imagined that it might be snowing in there, or perhaps a hailstorm was pummelling the grass where the girl sat, waiting it out. Because the girl played under a boundless sky in there, which in many ways was the same sky that lay so lightly over Lydia and over Edvin, over their sleep, their daily life. What whims! No, no, she really must stop this, she had to get a grip and be done with it. But these imaginings came from a seemingly inexhaustible source, and they amused her and definitely made the waiting less wearisome. The girl fought valiantly to be alive, struggled through dense scrub, pushed branches aside, got closer. It was a time of anticipation. There were only short periods of anxiety when Lydia thought there was something dark hanging over her and the child. She could wake up suddenly in the middle of the night and listen frantically for the heartbeat. It was so transparent, not as direct and palpable as her own, and then she sometimes called on all the good forces, she might even whisper to the unborn child that she had to hold on until the very end. It was only natural that she was afraid that something unspeakable might happen, that something dreadful might happen to the tiny being, because then everything else in Lydia would be extinguished too, then Edvin would find her charred in the bed beside him. These were her thoughts, and so she continued to think, until it was nearly the end of July and time to honour Saint Olav, and thus also time for the birth.

NAMED
THINGS

First she buttoned up her blouse, which was tight over her belly, and then she went to the door.

In the middle of the day when the light streamed in, the room always looked somewhat abject, despite the poppies in the vase.

And the furniture, objects, and fabric slowly became worn, they faded and disintegrated, as though after exhausting work; but they were kept in the memory, where they were immortalized.

The red saucepan, for example, had been bought in town one day when it was raining.

Had she locked the door? Had she at least remembered to take the key?

A strong summer wind made the leaves on the trees dance, they looked like ships about to capsize. In her dream, she thought she no longer had confidence in the world.

She thought she should have taken with her something to read, a book or a magazine, but now it was too late, that is to say, she decided it was too late, even though she was only a few steps down the gravel path, and anyway, the taxi was already there waiting for her.

Edvin rang to say he was on his way, and she detected a strange tone in his voice.

The understanding between them held strong without promises, explanations, or secrets. As though the facts were enough in themselves.

And that they had shared interests.

The joy that can sometimes be derived from discussions that led to greater understanding.

The yellow indicator on the local bus was barely visible in the sunlight. She closed her eyes against the passenger window, against the forested hill, as though driving past entailed some kind of trap.

With the child in her belly, she thought about death, that it was getting closer, without warning. But she still saw herself in hospitable surroundings, candles were still lit in the rooms for a moment, and the shadows, with their lean limbs, lay down gently on top of her.

Her shoulders started to shudder.

And the blue tarpaulin over the pile of planks, it was not properly secured.

In one of Edvin's books, she had read, over his shoulder: "That which was new was so vague, so impossible to grasp."

The memories subside, the words are forgotten, a friendly gesture left behind, a loving gaze that withers.

As the taxi approached the hospital, she spotted a girl on a pedestrian crossing. She was sixteen, seventeen, and her oversized sunglasses made her look like an actress who wanted to hide her identity.

They could have talked about anything—English furniture design, for example.

And the child, all the habits, routines, all the trivial and monotonous things that made up a secure existence.

Nothing should be brown or ochre.

But what would the birth be like? How would things unfold? Perhaps she would have to half close her eyes because the sight was too powerful.

Unlike a mountain, the forest is forgiving.

The taxi driver accompanied her all the way to the elevator. The maternity ward was on the second floor. Another woman was there for the same reason. They looked each other up and down, smiled cautiously, observing each other. Lydia thought the woman was incredibly elegant.

As though God had just seen through her. What nonsense, she was tired of thinking now.

Sometimes, in pressing situations, Lydia would stick her hand into her coat pocket as though looking for a cigarette, but she had no cigarettes, she had never smoked.

She lost herself in dreams: the sound of a pigeon flying up from the bracken. She was a child, and like a child, she walked into a forest.

Daniel in the lion's cave. To prove what?

In the hawthorn thicket, an insect landed on a leaf, full of a strange kind of tenderness. What then became visible and what ceased to be were related. And the fact that she listened, that she registered, what was so close. What was barely visible.

In her childhood: the puddles glittered, the small pools presented themselves in the sun. Horses in the vicinity of the clouds.

And a cloud of pollen drifting over the graveyard.

Do you like the sour gooseberries? her mother asked.
Yes, Lydia replied.
Nor do I, said her mother.

And when the calf was finally released and slipped out, it fell down hard onto the straw, and her hands were sticky with blood that steamed in the cold air, as though her fingers were breathing.

Edvin whispered that he was overjoyed about the child, not in her ear, but against her mouth, as his lips brushed hers.

The bed linen would smell freshly ironed. Then she would, without any mind games, surrender herself to him.

Or she lay completely still and pretended to sleep.

Faithless.

In a dream, the child came wandering out of the sun.

The simplest solution.

In front of her, doors opened.

All the unavoidable mistakes.

And in an unnaturally extrovert manner, she mumbled: See how attentive the world is.

The light blinded her. A dark negative. And the birth dazzled her. And she who thought she heard a rare bird sing.

In welcome: the baby girl with her thin, delicate limbs.

Time, which had stopped for a short while, now continued undaunted, only to stop again. And eclipsed by summer, the child sprouted, grew there in the shadow, illuminated.

And the unknown child's unknown face—familiar in glimpses, like a reflection, but unclear.

The rest can be said in few words.

She was not quite herself.

SHE HEARD
THE ANIMALS TALK

On her way to the delivery room, with a nurse a short step in front of her, Lydia had felt the hot wind blowing in through an open window, and yet a couple of hours later, in the midst of all the strain and pain, which was far worse than she had imagined, for some peculiar reason she suddenly thought it was raining outside; she lay and listened to a heavy and persistent rain, as though she needed something imagined and paradoxical to hold on to in order to circumvent the pain, and so in the weeks that followed she remembered the cloud burst, the water that washed over the asphalt and lawns.

The child slept for the most part. And yet the first weeks were spent awake, keeping watch. Edvin had carried the small cot into the bedroom. And he sat and talked nonsense to the little one, and only when she had fallen asleep did he come and lie close to Lydia, his strong hand lightly on her buttock, tired caresses before he too drifted off to sleep. Lydia herself lay there and listened to her daughter's breathing. The steady, almost inaudible inhale and exhale only made her more alert. She tried to read to lull herself to sleep, but her lack of concentration made it an irritating and inexpedient sleeping aid, and Lydia did not settle until dawn was on its way. By then she was so knocked out that she did not even register Edvin leaving: the click of the front door, his footsteps on the gravel, the car starting. But the slightest whimper from the little girl was enough to get her out from under the duvet. She went for long walks with this tiny new being. The shifting autumn air was waiting for them. And she would chat to this person and that, people she barely knew: along the road, in the shop, at the baker's; small girls, the postman, women she had never exchanged a word with before, some farmer she had once visited to examine a bull, a calf. And then she heard about a boy from the next village who had died of croup. Croup? Could that really happen? On the way home she had to stop, simply to breathe. The girl lay in the carriage, the sunbeams filtered through the leaves and danced on her still-indistinct face. Lydia lifted her out of the carriage. She kissed her soft forehead and whispered that she would be called Dagmar. It was as though Lydia was impatient to get to know her. She pictured the poor boy lying there gasping and wailing, perhaps for even several nights in a row. Now he was erased, lost, gone. We are reluctant to use the word *dead* when children are nearby, and if asked about the fate of a child or a young person, in particular, we generally put on a flat and measured expression; nothing to worry about, we say. Because what else can one say about death? It is as though, if one gives it life, and one does whether one wants to or not, it carries with it an undefined hunger, a great, insatiable loneliness. But it is neither terrible nor cunning, simply helpless, and therefore also merciless.

She pulled herself together, pulled up her socks, so to speak, decided, as if a decision were possible, that this was not a gruelling time; the girl's breath on her cheek filled her with expectation, as did the sun that blazed through the branches, and the spiky horse chestnuts that more or less covered the ground where she stood. She thought that her father should call her. He should call her and say how much he longed to see her, her and the child. What was he doing back there on the farm? The meagre harvest? Keeping the wisteria alive? It would manage by itself. What was it about isolation that was so intoxicating?

Back at the house, Lydia stopped and once again lifted the girl up from the carriage. She pointed at the trees and said "trees," she said "house," "garden," and "clouds," simple things that had not been robbed of their easily understood meaning. She remembered that her father had once broken a tooth. He had been eating a plum, and a piece of the stone had split his tooth all the way up to the gum. Lydia could imagine, without any problem, that it must have hurt like hell. His mouth filled with blood, which he spat into the grass, then came the curses, the oaths: hell and damnation, over and over again. Lydia was just a child. She had no idea what the words meant. But it was more than a little frightening to see her father like this, mutilated and furious like a wounded lion attacking its poor prey. Dagmar put him in his place, he should not call on the devil, because that was what he was doing, she believed, not in front of her, and certainly not in front of his daughter. No, he could do better than that, a grown man. And Johan restrained himself, spat once again, and went to get a bottle of brandy from the kitchen cupboard, took a slug, swilled it around his mouth, and spat it out again, as though to demonstrate to his wife and child that he was no drunkard, he certainly did not need any stimuli to dull the pain. He put the cork back in the bottle and left it on the garden table, lifted Lydia up in his arms, and apologized, because it was true, one should never call on the devil, it never led to any good, and Lydia tried to look pious and forgiving, even though she was sure the devil did not exist, so his oaths would come to nothing. In a disguised attempt to get a peep at the broken tooth, she stared at her father's mouth, and he noticed and opened his mouth wide, let her touch the jagged tooth with her finger, then he put her down and opened his hand, and there was a piece of the bloodied tooth, and if she wanted it, she could have it.

The little girl fell asleep as soon as she was put down on the bed. She lay on her back with her arms and legs out in every direction. There was an open book lying on the sofa. Both pages showed ancient illustrations of the seven hills of Rome, the proportions were very odd, Lydia thought. She lay down on the sofa with her head toward the baby. She held her hands up in front of her. Her fingers were long and slim and had a healthy roughness. She caught the scent of wet grass. She thought about Lise, the woman from Antwerp. Was her name not Lise? Lise walked across the room. She leaned over, unabashed, her mouth close to Lydia's ear, an intimacy that was in no way uncomfortable. And she had a book in her hands. Did she want to show Lydia something? A picture, a paragraph? Lydia raised herself up onto her elbows to see better, so she could see both the woman and the book, but then the dream evaporated and she was alone. Rome's seven hills lay on the floor. Alone. She got up, checked on the child, whose breathing was calm and steady. She went into the kitchen and made a cup of tea. And as she drank the warm brew, she experienced a kind of delayed feeling of having been indiscreet. Was it a suppressed desire that had surfaced? Not at all. Indeed, it was more a whim than a love scene. She was perhaps a little restless, and restlessness often gives rise to curiosity, one opens oneself to all manner of probable and improbable situations. It was harmless enough. Lydia thought, with some humour, that all the restlessness had something to do with the asymmetrical relationship between mass and energy. She finished her tea and went back into the living room, where the baby was still asleep. Soon the girl would grow, Lydia thought. Soon she would be able to take her for walks and show her the animals, all the creatures that her daughter would learn to love. Then she would point at a horse and say "horse," and a bull would be called "bull," and together they would repeat the sounds that the animals made. And Dagmar would be called "Dagmar," and the name would have its own demands and its own stories. They would listen to the owl, and the frogs by the pond, and the silence of the bats in the gloaming. She would no doubt learn to appreciate the whistling of the birds, the monotone melody of the crickets, and the buzz of the bumblebees in the cornflowers.

ONE DAY SHE WALKED
IN THE DIRECTION
OF A FOREST

Anna Schou only managed to meet Dagmar once before she died. When December came knocking again, Lydia took her daughter with her to the house in the forest, and one of the first things Anna said was that Dagmar was a rare name these days, but she thought it had a distinguished ring to it, an echo from younger years, from her early childhood, because, as far as she could remember, she had had a nanny called Dagmar, and this nanny—imagine, that they had actually had something like that—had been a reliable and loving person. And then Anna died. Only a few days after their visit, she passed quietly on, and it was a sad loss for Lydia, as though she had lost a close friend. And a week later, she stood in the graveyard, in the cold, and threw flowers down on the coffin. She stood there with Brandt and a handful of local people. It was a miserable advent, their first with a child. All the small and normally joyful things somehow seemed empty now: the cartoons on TV, the food, the music, all the riches that Lydia and Edvin carried with them from childhood. And this special period that had previously brought them peace now seemed more like a slightly anxious shove toward the

New Year. But then, the day before Christmas Eve, the mood lifted. It was as though Lydia's despondency was such a stark contrast to the little girl, who was totally unaware of what was casting the long shadows. Fortunately, Dagmar was not a demanding child. She slept from early evening to late morning, she ate her food with great dexterity, and looked extremely well on it. The rest of the Christmas celebrations were like a quiet eruption of gratitude. Every evening, Edvin and Lydia could watch a film in peace, or they collapsed side by side onto the sofa and chatted, made love, fell asleep intertwined in bed. For a while, they abandoned themselves to intimacy. The tenderness of their relationship was built on a heart-to-heart understanding rather than constant and intense elaborations of emotions and inner affairs. Lydia was not the shy type. She could be reserved and reticent, it was true, but she gave herself willingly to Edvin, it was like a favour that cost her nothing, it was like sharing a handful of wild strawberries picked on a sunny slope. The first time she got involved in an erotic relationship, it was with a boy in her class at high school, and in some inexplicable way it seemed to be something already familiar to her, something she had experienced before, and she remembered every episode and meeting in detail.

On New Year's Day, she woke and knew immediately, before she had even rubbed the sleep from her eyes, that she was alone in the room: no light breathing from the cot, no mumbling from Edvin. She got out of bed. She heard noises from the kitchen, voices whispering. She stopped to listen. Was that her father talking? Yes, it was her father talking. She quickly patted down her hair and went in. Why had they not woken her? Well, they had decided to let her sleep. She needed it, Johan said. But what a blessing the child was, and that they had chosen to call her Dagmar. Yes, Dagmar really was the right name for her. Lydia's father gave her a hug. He was clearly moved. Eivor had driven him all the way to Trondheim, he told them, and then he had taken the train from there. He should, of course, have told them he was coming, but it had been on such an impulse—he wanted now to see how Lydia lived in Norway and he had her address, after all. Edvin made coffee, a big pot, but Johan was very tired, so if it was not inconvenient, he would appreciate a few hours' sleep. Lydia went to make up a bed for him in the guest room straightaway. For a brief moment, as she tucked the sheet in under the mattress, she was about to accept his credible explanation but then was gripped by anxiety. The impulsive journey was the sort of thing one might embark on if one had only a short time left to live. What a cynical thing to think. It was as though she no longer saw him as her father, but as a stranger who had come to the door with something he wanted to sell. Something useless and unwanted but that one gave some money for all the same, alms of a sort, paltry, of course, but then that was the purpose of money. She turned on the bedside lamp, then pressed down the door handle with care, as though reluctant to wake herself from the surrealness of those first hours of the New Year.

Later in the morning, she listened at the door of the room where Johan was resting. She heard snoring and tiptoed away again, relieved to have heard a sign of life. Edvin wanted to know what she was doing. He found it hard to believe there was anything wrong with his father-in-law. Naturally his age had an impact, but the man seemed both fit and well.

Edvin took Dagmar out into the snow-covered garden. Lydia studied them through the window. Edvin stood with the wrapped-up little girl in his arm. He talked to her. The distance in time made it difficult for Lydia to make the connection between her mother and her daughter, who were united by their name. But she remembered with great clarity what she thought on those stormy evenings in her childhood when her mother came in to close the window. They said goodnight, and Lydia lay there in the fitful dark, blinded by fantasy, and dreamed about ghosts and the undead who prowled around in the storm.

Johan appeared again later on in the evening, and Lydia heated up the leftovers from their New Year meal. Her father was delighted to be served what he called a good winter meal: salted lamb ribs, mashed turnip, pickled cabbage, and golden waxy potatoes. And out of the blue, while helping himself to the food, he started to talk about the inheritance that Lydia could expect, because it was not only the farm, there was also some money, not much, but what little he had saved over the years. Lydia felt that what was linked to an unspecified point in the future was now getting disagreeably close. She felt so awkward in this confrontation with the inevitable. There were no colours or nuances in the word *inheritance*, she thought. Was he ill after all? She asked him straight out why it was so urgent to talk about these things. She used the expression *these things*. And with a cunning kind of pedantry, he said that when it came to money, it was important that everything was in order and that prospects were clear. Lydia was tempted to tell him to get lost, but Edvin pushed his foot against hers under the table, as though to warn her to keep quiet. And with the greatest ease, Johan changed the subject. He wanted to know how things were, with the child and work and everything. He seemed to be genuinely interested, keen to know. The evening passed in a good-humoured openness. But that night, Johan Erneman died. Edvin had been woken by his laboured breathing. He made a hot toddy, which he insisted Johan should drink. And while they waited for the doctor, Lydia sat silently beside the bed and watched her father. It looked as though an unexpected trust had filled his old, defiant heart. Lydia thought that when he woke, he would be pleased to see her there and would ask, bewildered, if he had been asleep for a long time.

THE WALLPAPER DOOR

After the funeral, several months passed before Lydia could face travelling north again; her mother and father lay in the same grave. She regretted that she had not said yes when Edvin suggested they go together this time too. He would gladly have taken time off to do it. But Lydia had insisted on going alone. She wanted Edvin and Dagmar to stay at home. She needed to spend a few days alone on the farm, needed to open the door to her childhood home without having to think about anything other than her own feelings and emotions. She let herself in, and what was once a playground, a living farm and a dream, was now empty and abandoned. She regretted her decision. Edvin could have been here with her. He could have held her in his arms and said that everything would be tidied and washed and sorted, that it was no big deal, that the grass would soon be cut and in a moment the house would smell of freshly made coffee. The air around the small farm was thick with pollen and the fine rain had the sour smell of chlorophyll. Once the snow had melted later than usual, only the wind and first cold spring rain had prevented the grass and weeds from reaching up toward the sky.

Lydia felt in her coat pockets for the key. Her hand was trembling and continued to do so as she let herself in. It was as though she had come home without warning, after a long life lived abroad. She was the prodigal daughter who had disappeared off to Minneapolis or Canberra or Winnipeg when she was young, and no one had heard from her since. She gave herself a moment before going in to get used to the dimness and heavy smell. The house had been shut up all through the long winter. It reeked of ash and oil and dust that had been allowed to settle. Everything was where it should be: her father's chair, the hunting rifle over the fireplace, the bureau in the hallway, the enamel dish, and the key.

Out in the kitchen, Lydia stood still and listened. Fat flies buzzed half-heartedly against the window or crawled without heed over or around their dead relations. She continued on into the living room. A sense of foreboding hung in the darkness of the room. Did the old gramophone player still work? She plugged it in and turned it on. A small green light appeared and the needle hit the vinyl with a dry click, a sound she had always liked. And then there was Vivaldi's Cello Sonata in A Minor. She knew it so well, turned up the volume, hummed along, conducted lightly with her right hand. She had never spoken about music with her father, nor with her mother, for that matter. They were not wont to say anything about what they valued in their family. But ever since Lydia was a little girl, the small record collection had been well used, and Lydia could remember that her mother, on one of her trips to Stockholm, had bought a new needle, a diamond needle. Diamond needle: it sounded so extravagant. But they never expressed their love of this or that piece of music by Vivaldi or Haydn or Bach. What was it her mother used to say? That openness deserved openness in return, and that what was closed also deserved to be met with openness. Lydia was never quite sure what the complicated saying meant, something tolerant and conciliatory, of course, as it was her mother's gentleness that spoke, it was her signature, so to speak, always soft and vague—Bible quotes or things she had made up herself, things that sounded like they should be quotes from the Bible.

The girl's room was damp. The latch on one of the windows had never been good and must have been shaken loose in a storm, as the window stood wide open with broken glass all over the floor. It was as though a harbinger of doom had been there and left a message. Lydia had planned to make up the bed in here so she could sleep in her old room at night, but now she had to abandon that. She decided to sleep in the car instead. There was a sleeping bag in the closet down the hall. She shook it out and left it to air on the front step. Went to the car, pushed back the passenger seat, pushed down the back as far as it would go. The spring evening was waning. The air was still and cold. The mountainside to the east lay pale in the mist. She sorted herself out and turned on the car radio to keep her company, flicked on the headlights for a moment. The beam flared up and the front of the house emerged fleetingly from the dark, as though new rooms had opened up inside, new hallways and stairs with landings she had never trod before.

Early the next morning, she woke from a nightmare. It was half past four. She found it hard to breathe. She could not remember much of what she had dreamed, but one image had burned itself into her memory: a face, an unknown man's face, with hundreds of small eyes bearing down on her. And was there not a voice as well? No, she could not remember a voice, nothing was said. To shake off the discomfort, she went into the house and started to clear up. She was efficient and unsentimental in her pursuit, throwing away all manner of old rubbish; anything she thought there and then was of no value she carried out and piled up in the yard, without too much thought, without acknowledging what might at some point in the future arouse sweet memories. Wall lights, standard lamps, small mounted shelves, carpets and tablecloths and kitchen utensils, chairs and side tables—in fact, nearly all the furniture was carried, pulled, and pushed out through the narrow doorway, out into the morning sun. To a passerby, it would look like she was preparing an enormous midsummer bonfire. She noticed how good it felt to use her muscles again, it had been a while since she had tussled with cattle and horses, and she was happy to feel her limbs aching from all the effort. She filled a bucket with boiling, soapy water and started to scrub down the rooms, and was thorough and systematic here too: one room at a time from floor to ceiling, upstairs first. She had to change the water frequently. She went over all the walls and floors twice, and in the living room, where the open fire had spewed out ashy smoke for years, she was not content until she had gone over all the surfaces with a coarse cloth four times.

As she worked, it struck her just how often she had felt out of sorts and downcast in her childhood home. And the thought filled her with sadness, it was like a weight, it fell over her like a wet cloth on a line or falling snow that blankets what only minutes before had been a green garden full of flowers. There she stood facing furniture and objects from an abandoned past life; the flower vase whispered, the brown coat stand spoke of its experiences, the hat shelf with its rusty screws mumbled its stories, and her father's well-worn clothes all talked at the same time. Innumerable descriptions, occurrences, and events that had made up daily life on the old farm, nothing had gone unnoticed. And even though nothing was irrelevant, even though nothing was silent, there was nothing to be done; all of it had to go, she would not spare anything.

As she washed over the walls in her parents' bedroom with a damp cloth, she discovered a hidden door behind the dry, faded pale purple wallpaper. She traced the barely noticeable crack with her fingertips, went out into the hall, counted her footsteps, measured with outstretched arms. The hidden room could not be much bigger than two or three square metres. She stood in front of the wall and studied the rectangular area that was now visible to her. She was curious and yet inclined to let the room go unexplored, as though she were reluctant to take on the role of plunderer. She put her ear to the wall and listened. A doorway to death, she imagined, into the dead. If they were not aware that they could no longer speak, would they then start to talk again? As though she had in some way managed to free herself from a trap, Lydia left the wallpaper door unopened.

Downstairs, in the kitchen, she found a bottle with a little vodka left in the bottom. She drank it in one go, relished the clean, neutral taste, and put the empty bottle in a plastic bag. She went outside and sat down in one of the armchairs. Of all things, she felt relieved, a kind of happiness, as though something depressing had let go. She remembered the first meeting with Edvin, recalled that at the time he had rather awkwardly complimented her by saying she was like Ingrid Thulin, albeit Ingrid Thulin dressed as Manda Vogler disguised as Mr. Aman. As though it were possible to fool someone into thinking Ingrid Thulin was a man. That was what was so good about watching films: one could so easily imagine that reality was like this or that, that there were other more hopeful and complicated possibilities in the world, as though the moving images, even those in black and white from a bygone era, proved this. She pulled the old mirror out of the "moving pile." The sunlight blinded her as she leaned it back against the worn leather sofa. Her face was completely clear in the mirror. Yes, she was beautiful. It was as though everything around her let out a muffled echo, a barely audible note. She thought about her daughter. There was a strange pureness and wholeness in what she felt for her. And this pureness, this wholeness, was unlike anything she could feel for a man, or for a woman, for that matter; no, what she felt for Dagmar was so utterly selfless.

SEVEN YEARS LATER

They walked through the forest, Lydia and Dagmar. Their walk had no purpose, other than to be out and moving in the fresh air, to smell the scent of the tangy pine trees and steaming forest floor. They had walked for an hour or so over the uneven ground, and down in the narrow gulley they had to pick their way through, it was so dark it seemed that time had confused day and night. But soon they emerged into a clearing, thin beams of light penetrated through leaves, and out on the open slope they saw a deer. They came upon the elegant creature so suddenly that they both held their breath. Dagmar took her mother's hand and they hunkered down between the trees. Fortunately the wind direction was in their favour. The deer stood grazing on a grassy tussock. Every now and then it lifted its head and sniffed the air, before carrying on eating without fear. Dagmar's eyes and mouth were open. Children and animals, Lydia thought, what a blessed instinct. And in that instant she pictured her daughter in a future existence, an existence where she herself had withdrawn, she was no longer alive. "May God protect you," she whispered, and "Godspeed," as though suddenly everything was at stake, as though it was imperative to pray that the girl would pull through, alive and well. From what? One must leave the best of oneself behind, Lydia thought. One must leave behind something that is simple and easy to disregard: not a ruby ring or expensive heirloom, no, nothing overbearing, but rather something mundane; a key in an enamel dish, a pile of science books, or a song once learned by heart. Yes, what is handed on should be ordinary and solid, something that can be easily used or discarded, like a peaceful conversation at dusk, like her mother's grey coat, something one can ruin or learn to love, like a small object one might put under one's pillow or pack away and forget without qualm.

They stayed where they were in the undergrowth until the deer was contented and bounded back into the forest. The gentle, barely audible sound of the hooves on the forest floor could be heard for no more than a moment, then there was silence, and Lydia and Dagmar stood up and turned back toward the car. Soon after, they drove through a dark concrete tunnel. An acrid dust was sucked in through the vents, which they had closed to no avail. When they finally emerged into daylight again, Dagmar rolled down the passenger window to let in some air. Her hair fluttered in the wind, whipped her eyes. She closed them, her mouth half open. She wanted to know if killing deer was allowed. She had a guarded look in her eyes. Could a hunter shoot their deer? Lydia had no option other than to nod in confirmation. No sooner had she expressed the sad truth than the phone rang, it was Brandt, he asked her to go to a farm where they had a half-dead cow in the stream.

The farmer, a thin, weathered man in his fifties, was standing waiting when they pulled into the yard. He took them over a field and down a small bank to the stream. The cow must have ventured too far down the slope and slipped. Now it was lying with its body in the brown water and its head twisted up against the wet grass on the bank. The man looked desperate. Like a sleepwalker, he took Lydia's coat and then stood tall and stooped beside Dagmar. Lydia had to wade out with the water to her knees in order to examine the poor beast properly. She opened its eyes, they shone white in the sun. She got out a stethoscope, crouched down, pressed the bell against its body, and listened, felt its belly. She asked the farmer to pass her bag to her. Lacteal fever, she said, more to herself. The animal needed calcium. She found what she needed and injected an intravenous dose, then waited a short while before she listened with the stethoscope again. She lay down over the animal. The water splashed against her stomach and ran under the waistband of her trousers. The sound of the heart was clearer now. Systole and diastole, she mumbled, as though she was back in Ultuna, as keen and methodical as a novice. Another dose was injected, and again Lydia waited for the remedy to take effect. Then they had to get the cow to its feet. The farmer, who had been standing as though bewitched, woke up and ran to get help, and not long after returned with three men at his heels. They worked efficiently, even Dagmar gave a hand, and soon the cow was standing in the water again. It staggered up the bank and started to lurch about. At one point it looked as though it might kneel, that it would collapse in a daze, but it kept on moving with drawn-out, tottery steps at blessed intervals. And then it was done, the exertion was over. The farmer could not thank Lydia enough. She had woken the cow from the dead, he said. He took Lydia's bag, grabbed Dagmar's hand, and they walked together across the field toward the farmhouse. He took a wooden crate, the kind used for berries and fruit, from one of the storehouses and then invited them into the house, into the kitchen. There was a delicious scent of apples, of harvest. He filled the crate with a fresh loaf of bread, two bottles of apple juice, various vegetables, two dozen eggs, and as though that was not enough, he topped it all with a cake that smelled of butter and lemon. He said very little but carried these delights out to the car and gave both Lydia and Dagmar an awkward but sincere hug. Lydia started the car, relieved at the happy outcome.

The next day was also busy. As Edvin was rehearsing a new play in town, and Dagmar was on her autumn break, Lydia took her to work again, after an early breakfast. They drove into the low sun. A combine harvester was blowing up the dust in one of the fields, two horses galloped down toward the river where the trees provided shade, and on the far side of a patchwork of fields, the local train cut through the landscape.

Soon Dagmar welcomed her first calf, it fell wet and sticky onto her, but she helped it up without hesitation. She led it to the bursting udder and stood holding her breath as she watched the greedy and eager creature. And later on in the afternoon, on the way home from a job well done, Lydia stopped the car at the side of a paddock. A herd of cows was running with the sun. Dagmar climbed up and sat on a fence post. She looked like she had something on her mind, but it was equally clear that she did not know where to start. Lydia studied her or, rather, watched her in secret. Her daughter reminded her of something she had once read: Tell me, my pretty one, what were you doing on the roof today? Looking where the wind blows from. Why? Whence the wind blows, thence blows happiness. Indeed were you invoking happiness by song? Where there is song, there is also good fortune. Supposing you sing in grief for yourself? What of it? What is your name, my nightingale? Whoever named me knows. And who named you? How should I know?

NOTES

The quote "Silence falls on the vale..." is taken from the poem "Aftonfrid" by Jacob Tegengren (1875–1956). The *Old Farmer's Almanac* is a series of books with seasonal content and weather forecasts. The first of its kind was the German *Die Bauern-Praktik* (1508). The words of wisdom and weather sayings have made little impact on folk traditions in Norway, whereas they have long been deeply rooted in Sweden. The poem "Outside the Summer Wind Blows" was written by Samuel Hedborn (1783–1849). The text "From the hill, where the unassuming, yet ancient and inviting church stood..." is taken from the book *Arbetets söner—Et illustrationsverk öfver den svenska arbetsklassen* (1906). "My home is so humble..." is taken from the poem "Mitt hem" by Carl Rupert Nyblom (1832–77). The quote "Are you so poor, wee darling..." is taken from the poem "Ett litet öde" by Johan Ludvig Runeberg (1804–77). The quote "But what she wants is nothing more or less than a miracle..." is taken from the novel *Farmor och vår Herre* (1921) by Hjalmar Bergman (1883–1931). The first paragraph in the chapter "Short

Intermission" is a paraphrase of the opening of *Familien på Gilje, et Interieur fra Firtiaarene* (1883) by Jonas Lie (1833–1908). "There is a gravity that comes from the earth…" is an untitled poem from the collection *I de mörka rummen, i de ljusa* (1976) by Bo Carpelan (1926–2011). The quote "That which was new was so vague…" is from the novel *Things* by Georges Perec (1936–82). The final dialogue is an adaptation of a conversation taken from *A Hero of Our Time* (1840) by Mikhail Lermontov (1814–41). Unless otherwise stated, the translations of all these quotes are the translator's own.

ACKNOWLEDGEMENTS

From the Author:
I would like to express my gratitude to Hazel and Jay Millar at Book*hug Press, to Kari Dickson for her dedicated work with the translation, to Henrik Francke at Oslo Literary Agency for his tireless work, and to Cathrine Narum, my editor at Forlaget Oktober.

From the Translator:
My thanks to Rune Christiansen and everyone at Book*hug Press. It is wonderful to work with all of you.

ABOUT THE AUTHOR

Rune Christiansen is a Norwegian poet and novelist. One of Norway's most important literary writers, he is the author of more than twenty books of fiction, poetry, and non-fiction. He has won many prestigious awards, including the 2014 Brage Prize for his bestselling novel, *The Loneliness in Lydia Erneman's Life*. *Fanny and the Mystery in the Grieving Forest* was shortlisted for the same prize and published in English by Book*hug Press in 2019. He is also a professor of creative writing. Christiansen lives just outside of Oslo, Norway.

ABOUT THE TRANSLATOR

Kari Dickson is a literary translator. She translates from Norwegian, and her work includes literary fiction, children's books, theatre, and non-fiction. In 2019, Book*hug Press published her translation of Rune Christiansen's *Fanny and the Mystery in the Grieving Forest*, and, in 2021, her co-translation of Mona Høvring's *Because Venus Crossed an Alpine Violet on the Day that I Was Born*. She is also an occasional tutor in Norwegian language, literature, and translation at the University of Edinburgh, and has worked with the British Centre for Literary Translation and the National Centre for Writing. Dickson lives in Edinburgh, Scotland.

Colophon

Manufactured as the first English edition of
The Loneliness in Lydia Erneman's Life
in the spring of 2023 by Book*hug Press

Copy-edited by Stuart Ross
Proofread by Charlene Chow
Type + design by Ingrid Paulson
Cover images ©iStockPhoto

Printed in Canada

bookhugpress.ca